THE
STEP
CHILD

BOOKS BY NICOLE TROPE

THE
STEP
CHILD

NICOLE TROPE

bookouture

Published by Bookouture in 2022

An imprint of Storyfire Ltd.
Carmelite House
50 Victoria Embankment
London EC4Y 0DZ

www.bookouture.com

ISBN: 978-1-80314-261-6
eBook ISBN: 978-1-80314-260-9

For Isabella
The reader who is becoming the writer

PROLOGUE

The child is still, her eyes closed, dark lashes brushing pale cheeks. Small hands, little fingernails painted in a vivid blue with a single gold stripe down the centre of each, lie slack on the ground. In the surrounding bush of the park, magpies call to each other, a pair of rainbow lorikeets flit from tree to tree and a lone rabbit halts its movement on hearing a sound, remaining frozen in place as it waits for silence to return. There's a cool wind and heavy grey clouds obscuring the sun; winter is still here, despite spring being only days away.

The little girl is dressed in pink corduroy dungarees with a thick blue top underneath. Matching pink suede Ugg boots complete the outfit. Fine black hair fans out from her head, covering the grey-brown dirt she's lying on. The clearing is tucked away at the side of the park – a cold corner where the grass refuses to grow.

There are a couple of people walking their dogs in the park, but the owner of the brown and white collie is only concerned with looking for his pet's favourite green ball. He threw it and somehow the dog can't seem to find it. He peers through trees and around bushes, but he's not getting on his knees to try and locate the silly thing. He has spares at home. The owner of the German shepherd is looking for a tap so she can give her dog some water. She knows there's one somewhere in the park but she can't remember where.

No one is looking for a little girl. Not yet.

Later, the sun will be out and families with small children finding ways to get through a Saturday afternoon will fill the park. Children will dart in and out of clearings, chasing each other and scrunching over the last dead leaves of the season. Concerned parents will follow and watch, not wanting to lose sight of their children in the large area.

'Don't go too far,' a woman will call.

'Stay where I can see you,' a man will shout.

But by that time, by the time the park is full of people who might look, people who might see, people who might do something... it will be too late.

CHAPTER ONE

LESLIE

1.30 p.m.

Leslie slides into the driver's seat of the grey Range Rover, enjoying the new-car smell that lingers on the maroon leather despite the car being months old. 'I don't need such an expensive car,' she had told Randall when he bought it, wanting her to have something equally as expensive as his sleek silver Jaguar and something that worked as a family car.

'But I want to buy it for you,' he'd replied. The car had been difficult to get used to – its size making Leslie nervous on the roads – but now she loves its quiet luxury, despite never having desired it in the first place.

She glances at her phone in her hand and shakes her head. 'Look at the time,' she mutters, shoving it in her bag.

As she starts the car, the phone rings and Leslie's heart sinks when she sees it's Shelby. The queues at the grocery store were longer than she'd expected, and she has been gone nearly two hours. She presses a button on her steering wheel to answer the call and then takes a deep breath and gets ready to apologise, thinking of something to promise her stepdaughter so that she will not be confronted with sulking rage for the rest of the weekend. A shopping spree on that website she likes? A chance to have the big television to herself all night? What will work? The options circle in her head. Shelby, at twelve, is proficient at a dropped lip, a heavy sigh, a slammed door. She makes her displeasure known to everyone in the house. But today Leslie doesn't blame her. She had promised to be quick.

'Listen, Shelby—' she begins before the girl can even speak.

'She's gone!' Shelby's voice is high and tinged with hysteria.

'What?' asks Leslie, unsure if Shelby is actually talking to her.

'She's gone, she's gone – Millie's gone,' Shelby cries, tears obvious in the choking way the words come out.

'What do you mean?' Leslie struggles to understand what Shelby has said as she concentrates on pulling out of her parking spot. She brakes as she spots a woman pushing her trolley behind her car. 'What do you mean, gone?' she yells, her voice carrying through the slightly open window and causing the woman to stop for a moment and look at her before she moves on. 'How can she be gone? Where is she? Have you looked for her? Have you looked?' She swings the car to the left and moves away. She's sure she's misheard. Millie must be hiding, must be somewhere. Three-year-old children don't just disappear.

'I went...' Shelby pauses, as though searching for what to say, and then speaks quickly, 'I went to the bathroom and she... I don't know, she must have just opened the front door and left, she just... walked out... and she... I've looked for her. I've looked for her everywhere and she's not here. She's gone.'

Leslie listens as Shelby subsides into sobbing. She moves her hands on the steering wheel, feeling them slip a little because she is boiling hot in the cold car, her heart racing, her mind whirring. *Millie is gone... She's gone... Millie is gone.*

'Leslie, can you hear me? Did you hear what I said?' Shelby

screeches, her distress at fever pitch. 'She's gone, Millie's gone.' Her voice rises higher and higher as Leslie feels her own throat close over.

She pulls out into traffic, her mind jumbled with images and sounds and the one word that she has heard but doesn't want to hear.

Gone.

CHAPTER TWO

SHELBY

She sits on the sofa with her arms wrapped around herself in an attempt to try and feel better. If she could, she would pull up the black hood on her jumper and tug it down over her face, shutting all of this out. The police are on their way. Her mother is on her way, her heavy sigh over the phone alerting Shelby to how irritating this whole situation is. Her mother prefers relaxing Saturday afternoons watching Netflix with Trevor as they sip wine and eat cheese and crackers.

Her father returned from his golf game after Leslie called him, soon after she arrived home, and is now scouring the neighbourhood, still dressed in his stupid white pants and pink and white checked shirt, knocking on doors and asking if anyone has seen Millie.

'Just tell me what happened,' he'd commanded as he entered the house, his phone in his hand.

'I went—' Shelby began.

'I told you, she's not here,' Leslie shouted. 'I've searched everywhere. Just go and look around the neighbourhood. I've called the police. I'll check the house again.'

Her father had nodded, and Shelby could see he was

grateful to be told what to do. It's easier to be told what to do than to have to think for yourself.

'Just stay there,' Leslie said to her firmly, pointing at the sofa. And so she did what she was told, while Leslie ran back and forth through the rooms of the house and into the garden, shouting for Millie again and again, then calling her father to ask if he had found anything. Shelby knows there is no point to any of this. She has stayed on the sofa, rocking slightly and wishing she was anywhere but here.

It's after 2 p.m. and the sun has finally emerged from behind the clouds, casting a bright light over everything, which feels all wrong because there shouldn't be blue sky outside. It should be raining, the sky noisy with claps of thunder and hail battering the windows. But instead, the wind has died down and the sun is warming the air as though this is just another ordinary Saturday near the end of winter.

Shelby keeps her eyes focused on her sneakered feet on the pale blue carpet. Leslie bought her the sneakers a couple of weeks ago, shelling out the money for something her mother considered a 'ridiculous extravagance', and Shelby loves the black shoes with pink sides. She can't look up, can't meet her stepmother's brown eyes. Leslie is pacing back and forth now as she waits for the police, and every now and again she looks at her stepdaughter, and Shelby can tell she is looking at her like she knows, knows without a shadow of a doubt, that this is all Shelby's fault. And she's right – it is.

Leslie's car is parked outside at an odd angle, the grocery bags still in the boot. Shelby had been standing at the front door when she screeched into the driveway. Without turning off the engine, Leslie leapt out and grabbed her by the shoulders, shouting, 'Where is she, where is my child?' In that moment, with her teeth bared, she had not looked like Leslie. Instead, her long dark hair and pale skin made her look like an angry witch, and Shelby was afraid. She had felt her body moving back and forth, heard her teeth click-clack together and seen the scrunched, panicked look on her stepmother's face. 'Please, Shelby,' Leslie had begged.

'I don't know, I looked for her. I looked everywhere but I can't find her,' her voice high and thin because she couldn't catch her breath.

Leslie had let go of her abruptly and run through the house, calling for Millie, while Shelby stood silent and desperate, her stomach cramping at the thought of Leslie's wasted effort. Millie was not in the house. She was not in the street.

Leslie had returned to the open front door, where Shelby stood frozen, unsure what to do, afraid to move. 'Explain to me what happened,' she had said, even as her hands were calling Shelby's father, her attention drawn to the phone as he answered. 'You need to come home now, Randall... I know, but listen, just listen. Millie's gone missing. Shelby was babysitting and she says Millie left, opened the front door and just left, and we can't find her. She's just... gone. Come home now. Should I call the police? Do I need to call the police?... Okay, yes, yes, I will.'

She had hung up the phone and Shelby had watched as she dialled triple zero with shaking hands. Leslie had been silent for a few seconds, her chest heaving and tears coursing down her face, before the call was answered. 'I need to report my child, my child is missing,' she'd said. And then she had walked away from Shelby as she listened and answered questions about Millie's age and their address and how long the little girl had been gone. Shelby had heard Leslie tell whoever she was speaking to that it was twenty minutes, making up the time on the spot, but she was wrong about that. Millie had been gone for nearly an hour by then, nearly an hour.

When Leslie got off the phone from the police, she stood in front of Shelby and took a deep breath. Shelby could see that she was trying to calm herself. Then she lifted her hand and said, 'Just explain it to me, Shelby, just explain exactly what happened.'

'I went upstairs to the bathroom. I was only gone for a minute and then I came downstairs and she had just disappeared. I left her sitting at her table but she must have opened the door, the front door.' Shelby had spat out her prepared explanation quickly. Clear now that she'd rehearsed it a couple of times in her head.

Leslie nodded while she spoke, listening for clues. 'I told the police she's been missing for twenty minutes; I mean, you called me ten minutes ago and I assumed... How long has she been missing for?'

'More than that,' Shelby had whispered, dropping her head.

'What?'

'I looked for a bit, I thought she was just being silly, hiding or playing or something. And then I realised she'd run away.' Even to her own ears, the excuse sounded pathetic, made up – a lie.

'Why would she do that?' shouted Leslie. 'She's never done that before. Why would she do that?' She seemed to be asking the question of Shelby, of herself, of the universe, as she looked up at the bright white ceiling of the entrance hall.

Shelby had only been able to shake her head as she pushed the truth far down inside her so that it would not accidentally spill out. Leslie had rubbed at her forehead and looked out through the open front door at the empty street. 'You need to turn off the car,' Shelby said softly.

'What?' Leslie had yelled, and Shelby pointed at the purring SUV so she didn't have to say anything else. Leslie walked out of the house to the car and turned off the engine, shut the car door. Shelby had followed her because she had no idea what else to do, and she opened her mouth to ask if Leslie wanted the shopping brought inside, because then at least she was being helpful, was doing something. But Leslie had just looked at her and said, 'Go inside,' in a tone Shelby had never heard her use before. She could feel the fury in the two words.

Now Shelby looks at her phone, which is clutched in her hand, a screen saver picture of her and Kiera pulling silly faces for the camera. It's 2.15. Time seems to be moving faster than it should and crawling along as well. Millie has been gone since... She needs to know a time, needs to be able to tell the police an exact time, because they will ask. She looks at her phone again. 1.15. She came downstairs at 1.15 and Millie was gone, the living room empty. She had given Millie an avocado sandwich for lunch. *Shit.* She was supposed to give Millie an avocado sandwich. Would Leslie notice that the avocado in the fruit bowl, the dark green avocado she had picked up before she left and pressed slightly at the top, saying, 'This is ripe. Can you make a sandwich for Millie for lunch if I'm not back by then?' – would she notice that the avocado was still there, still whole?

She could just go into the kitchen and throw it out, but what if someone caught her? *Millie didn't want lunch yet*, she rehearses in her mind. *Millie didn't want lunch and so I waited, and then I went upstairs to the bathroom and I came downstairs afterwards and she... was gone.*

Her father comes back into the house. 'No one's seen her,' he says, sweat making his face shine. 'I'll go out again. I'll go to the park.'

'Maybe wait for a bit?' says Leslie, her eyes on her phone. 'The police will be here in a moment.'

'I'll get a drink of water,' he says, heading to the kitchen. He doesn't look at Shelby and she wraps her arms tighter around her body. She is cold, numb, terrified, angry, sad. She is everything and nothing. She rocks a little more.

After all the shouting from Leslie, and then the yelling from her father, everything is eerily quiet now. The important calls have been made. The right people are on their way and there is nothing to do but wait. She is suspended in time, floating between the moment of only a few people knowing about Millie and everyone knowing about Millie. When the police come, will they look at her and know? Can police see a lie on your face? She once watched a documentary with her father about police interrogation techniques – at least, she was sitting next to him looking at her phone while he watched – and she remembers hearing that someone who is lying will often touch their face. She sits on her hands on the grey sofa, feeling the smooth suede under her fingers.

What have I done? What have I done? What have I done? The words go round and round with nowhere to land in her head.

She moves her feet on the carpet, creating a darker blue line as she pushes against it the way Millie likes to do with her hand. Millie loves the colours blue and gold. She loves to have her nails painted. She has a dimple on one cheek and eyes the same colour as Shelby's.

Millie... Millie loved the colours blue and gold. Millie is. Millie was.

Shelby is in hell.

CHAPTER THREE

RUTH

I fold the tea towel in half and then in thirds and then make a perfect square. Sighing with satisfaction, I place it on the pile at my side, biting down on my lip as it wobbles slightly. The pile is leaning against the wall, but as it has grown, from ankle to knee to hip to shoulder height, it's become less stable. I am folding the tea towels on the dining room table, inherited from my grandmother, with its beautifully carved legs and shiny wood veneer top. I glare at the pile of tea towels for a moment and wait to see what happens, but it seems to have stabilised.

I prefer my piles of things to be stable. All around me in this room are the neat stacks of my collections. Tea towels, books, local newspapers, plastic cups, extension cords, magazines, laundry baskets and so many other things. I am a collector of everyday items of ordinary usefulness, of unnoticed but needed objects. Someone – a therapist my mother made me see – once called me a hoarder, but I don't like to think of myself like that. I've watched the show where they film hoarders and then try to help them. Their houses are overflowing with filth and disorder and vermin. Their houses have cats and dogs wandering around, messing everywhere. My house, my home, is not like that. Everything is neat and clean and tidy, even if some of the rooms aren't able to be used because they are filled to the brim with my beautiful collections. I clean all the time, removing grime, restoring order, brightening the space. Each time I add to a collection or straighten a pile I feel the warm glow of safety around me.

From the outside, there is nothing to set this house apart from any of the others in the neighbourhood. A few suburbs away, large mansions are crowding out the old houses, looming over the streets and taking all the space, but in my suburb, sixty-year-old houses still sit side by side, part of, instead of overshadowing, the landscape. It's a small, weatherboard-clad house with a black-tiled roof and cream-coloured walls. My front garden is neatly paved, from the little metal gate to the door, although the grass is not as green as I would like it to be. My late grandmother's car, a yellow Beetle, sits in the driveway. I keep it in good running order, knowing that it is a safe way for me to get around when I must, absolutely must leave the house. The slight lavender scent of her perfume is still embedded in the seats, and I feel her in there with me when I use it.

Inside, the house is old, reflecting the fact that it too used to belong to my grandmother, but the funky green laminate kitchen could have been put in yesterday.

My grandmother was a stickler for maintenance and cleaning, and so am I. She didn't collect like I do, but the small living room is still dwarfed by her large glass and wood antique cabinet filled with porcelain figurines of clowns and animals. When she was alive, I would help her remove all the delicate ornaments from the cupboard and carefully run water over them to wash off the dust. Her hands were frozen into place by then, the arthritis crippling one part of her body at a time, but she still managed to look after herself. She would explain where she got each little figurine, telling me about her travels with my long-dead grandfather. She had a special love for anything to do with cats. I dislike cats. I would have a dog, but I don't think I could cope with the mess, so even though I long for one, I wouldn't want to end up resenting the poor creature. I watch shows about dogs and look at Facebook posts about them, and whenever I am feeling terribly sad, which is quite often, I know I can turn to the internet to cheer me up. Golden retrievers are my favourite, but I also like the small ones, like the fussy white poodle whose owner likes to dress her up.

My grandmother loved dogs as well, but after her little fox terrier died, she didn't have the heart to get another. She herself died twenty years ago, when I was just eighteen. I remember her as the picture of elegance, with long snow-white hair that she piled high on her head. She dressed in two-piece knitted suits every day and always wore the same string of pearls. My mother and I moved into her house when I was sixteen. If she had been in better health, if she had been stronger, I could have told her why I refused to leave the house, why I refused to attend school, why I had started my collections. But she was already weak and struggling and I knew she couldn't take on my problems as well as her own. I contented myself with visiting her in her room every afternoon and regaling her with stories from television that might make her laugh. I miss her constantly, and so I dust her cabinet every day, making sure the glass is clear and everything can be seen. It allows me to feel close to her. After I have done the cabinet, I move around the house cleaning everything else, a duster in my hand and music pounding in my ears. Latin dance music, filled with drums and whistles and beautiful voices that make me want to dance.

When I'm not cleaning, I try to maintain a calm and serene manner in everything I do, but there are moments when a memory surfaces, a piece of my life I wish I could erase, and the past that I hate rears up and demands to be noticed. When panic strikes and my breathing become erratic as my heart races, that's when my collections save me. I will push over a pile and get down on my knees to begin the neat stacking that I know will help. With each item stacked and each pile made, my breathing gets deeper and my heart slows. I suppose I could have turned to pills and endless therapy, but this is better, I think. I think it's better.

I pick up the last tea towel and fold it in half and then in thirds, and then I make it a perfect square and add it to the pile against the wall. I admire the collection of colours and patterns all merging into one tall tower of neat squares. I have stacked them five times now, stacked them, knocked them over, stacked them, knocked them over, and finally my breathing has returned to normal and in the cold room I feel the sweat drying on my body.

This was a bad one, but of course it would be after what happened. I'm glad I managed to stave it off until I got home, but once I was here with the door locked, the clutching feeling around my heart began and I knew I couldn't avoid it. I look at the pile of tea towels and raise my hand quickly, knocking them over once more, and then I start again. Six is a good number of times. Best to be absolutely sure it's finished, that the gut-churning panic has lost its hold on my body.

In half, in thirds, in a neat square.

What was done to me. What I've done to someone else. What must be done now.

CHAPTER FOUR

LESLIE

2.30 p.m.

Two constables arrive, their uniforms jarring in her house, a sight she never expected to see. One of them is an older man, with greying hair and a slight paunch, blue eyes and a bulbous nose bothered by red veins. He is accompanied by a younger man with a riot of tight blonde curls and green eyes, almost angelic-looking.

'I'm Constable Dickerson,' says the older man, 'and this is Constable Willow.' He points at the younger man, who nods and smiles.

'Leslie,' says Leslie. She indicates Randall and Shelby. 'And this is my husband, Randall, and my... stepdaughter, Shelby.'

Randall is slightly sweaty from running up and down the street calling for their daughter. His curly brown hair is sticking up and his glasses are smudged with fingerprints because he keeps touching them. He's changed clothes at least and is now in blue jeans and a navy-blue jumper that matches his eyes. She had laughed at him this morning when he got dressed for his golf game.

'You look ridiculous. I'm sure you don't have to dress that way to be taken seriously,' she had said.

'No, but this outfit always gets a laugh and then everyone relaxes, and when people are relaxed, the deal is almost done,' he'd replied, sitting next to her on the bed. 'Much planned for the day?' he asked, lightly stroking her arm.

'Oh, you know,' she had said, waving a hand in the air. 'Shopping.' He didn't need to know about anything else.

'I'll see you tonight for pizza and wine,' he'd said, and he had left, leaving her with her daughter and her stepdaughter and a day to navigate alone.

The constables ask them to all remain in the living room while they walk through the house, checking the spaces that have already been checked. She has no idea why, but they must know what they're doing.

'Please stay off your phones, if you don't mind,' says Constable Dickerson, and Leslie obligingly puts her phone into the pocket of her black jeans. She hadn't even realised it was in her hand.

While they wait, she paces the living room, counting the minutes. She wants to be out looking for Millie.

'Did she eat her lunch?' she asks Shelby, because she doesn't like to think of her child being hungry as well as lost. *Is she just lost? Lost, yes, just lost, which means she will soon be found.*

'She didn't want lunch,' says Shelby, her arms tightly wrapped around herself as though it's cold in the house, which, Leslie supposes, it is, because of the open front door. She herself is warm, her blood rushing around her body, her breathing faster than normal. She's never had a panic attack, but it feels like this must be what the start of one is like. She looks at Shelby, waiting for her to explain why Millie, a child who loves her food, hadn't wanted lunch, but Shelby is staring down at her feet. The thumping of footsteps upstairs is accompanied by the sounds of doors being opened and closed. *She's not there. I know she's not there.*

Constable Willow returns to the living room. 'Is there any way into the roof?' he asks Randall.

'I don't... Um, Les, do you know if there is a way in?' her husband asks her. He had very little to do with buying and renovating the house because he was mostly at work while Leslie dealt with the builders and the myriad of decisions needed to create their home. 'You've done a beautiful job,' he told her when they moved in, but she was aware that it didn't matter to him as long as she was happy.

'There's a spare room next to our bedroom and there's a door on one wall, behind a curtain, that opens into the roof,' says Leslie, 'but she won't be in there.' Millie is frightened of the door that leads into the slightly dank-smelling roof space, crowded with cables and tubing for the air conditioner, and she won't even go into the spare room because of it. 'There's a monster what lives there,' she has told Leslie seriously.

'There's not, I promise you there's not,' Leslie has always replied, but childhood fears are stubborn and Millie likes the door to the spare room to remain closed.

'Always good to check everywhere,' says the constable, and he disappears again, leaving the three of them in silence.

Randall is looking at his phone, and Shelby glances up at him and then takes her own phone out of her pocket, staring down at it.

'Shelby, please put your phone down,' Leslie says, and is grateful that Randall puts his away as well.

Shelby throws a scowl at her and Leslie looks out of the window of the living room to the front garden, where the sun is lending a shine to the perfectly green grass. She can feel Shelby's anger at her. She shouldn't have grabbed her by the shoulders when she arrived home, shaking her to get an answer; she shouldn't have introduced her as her stepdaughter even though that's what she is. She shouldn't have left her child alone with her. That's the biggest one. Because now her daughter, her three-year-old baby girl, is gone, missing. Shelby was supposed to be looking after her little sister. She was supposed to be taking care of her. Leslie's daughter is missing, but her step-daughter is here. The very wrongness of this causes Leslie to pull at her hair, ostensibly straightening it but subtly pulling out a few strands to twist around her fingers. 'You'll end up with no hair if you keep doing that,' she hears her mother say, and even though when the words were said, Leslie frowned and hated her mother, she wishes her here now. The fact that this is impossible allows her hand to stray up to her head again, tugging and pulling another few strands.

'All right then,' says Constable Dickerson, returning to the living room, followed by Constable Willow, 'let's go through this from the beginning.'

He picks up a leather dining chair from its position at the head of the dining room table and carries it back to the sofa, where he places it opposite Shelby, sitting down with a slight grunt. Constable Willow stands beside him, a little blue note-book and a black pen in his hands. If Leslie had to describe the way he looks, she would say 'eager' – as though this is quite exciting. She pulls another strand of hair and then she looks at Randall and he gives his head a little shake. He is next to Shelby on the sofa but he is watching Leslie. If he were standing next to her, he would gently pull her hand away from her hair. He knows the action means she's feeling anxious and out of control. And now she is also terrified and angry and ashamed and... She feels her hand move back to her hair and quickly clasps both hands together to stop herself.

'How old are you, Shelby?' asks Constable Dickerson, his voice holding none of the usual lilt people have when speaking to children.

'Twelve,' says Shelby, two bright pink spots flaring on her

cheeks at the full attention of all the adults in the room. She has the same pale blue eyes Millie has, both of them getting that from Randall, but she has thick wavy blonde hair from her mother. It hangs down her back in perfect layers. As a teenage girl, fighting fine hair that would only hang straight, no matter what she did, Leslie had envied girls like Shelby, with their seemingly effortless beauty. Shelby is tall and thin, like her father, and there have already been discussions about a modelling career. Her mother, Bianca, is keen to get her daughter into an agency, but Randall will not allow it. 'She's too young. You know what happens to young girls who get involved in the modelling industry.' He has been very firm about this, an unusual thing for him. He gives in to Bianca on everything, the guilt over her circumstances eating away at him. 'She made her choice,' Leslie tells him, but Bianca makes sure when she speaks to him that he is aware that her life is not as easy as it should be. She never fails to mention some bill she has to pay. Leslie only recently became aware that when she does this, Randall offers to pay it for her.

'She's remarried now,' Leslie had told Randall a couple of months ago. 'I'm sure Trevor would hate that you're basically paying his bills.'

'I won't do it any more now that she has him. It was just to... I hate to think of Shelby listening to her talk about not having enough money when I have the means to help.'

Leslie had left it at that. It's his money, and while their marriage makes it her money as well, she works and they have more than enough. It's the principle of the thing that bothers her. When Bianca and Randall divorced, she sent him an email in which she told him not to come crawling back to her when he couldn't pay his bills. The universe has a unique sense of humour.

Leslie would have thought that Shelby would push her father on the modelling agency, just as she does on curfews and homework and babysitting duties, but she doesn't. She seems less interested than her mother is, content to fill up her social media accounts with selfies, with pictures she controls on a platform where she has the ability to restrict who sees her and who doesn't. Perhaps the idea of casting calls and competition with other beautiful girls doesn't appeal to her, or maybe it is the unwanted attention that comes with having your face become public property that worries her.

'You have to get up so early and you can't eat any junk food at all, like ever. That would make me crazy,' she told Leslie and Randall over dinner one night. 'But I may decide to do it. I don't know.' Shelby's whole life stretches before her, filled with choices, because she is pretty and clever and her father has enough money to get her anything she wants. It's such a contrast to the way Leslie grew up – in a single-parent home with a mother who taught her that money was a precious resource, not to be wasted. Leslie's own father had a haphazard approach to child support and more often than not failed to pay what he was supposed to. Leslie also grew up believing herself to be below average in everything from looks to intelligence to sporting ability. Her mother worked hard to convince her otherwise, but Leslie preferred to be realistic, and she still does. Shelby is living a very different life to hers. She is a privileged child and very little is asked of her, and today all she had to do was take care of a three-year-old for a couple of hours. Leslie's hand strays up to her head again, the pull and sting of the few strands of hair coming away allowing her to pay attention to the constable.

'Right,' says Constable Dickerson to Shelby, 'can you tell me exactly what happened this afternoon?'

'I... um... I was babysitting Millie while Leslie was at the shops. She was only meant to be gone an hour but she was gone... longer than that,' the girl says.

Leslie jumps in, her justification bursting out of her. 'The lines were long and I didn't realise. It just took longer than I thought it would.'

Constable Dickerson turns around, his whole body moving in the chair. 'Right, thanks, I think we just need to hear from Shelby right now.' He looks at Leslie for a moment longer and she nods, biting down on her lip, suitably chastised.

Shelby's hands dance up and down her arms, pulling at the material of her black hoodie. 'She was gone for such a long time; way, way longer than she said she would be and I was *supposed* to be going out with my friend.'

Leslie nods again, agreeing with this, even though the constable is not looking at her. She is standing near the carved arch that leads into the living room from the entrance hall of the open-plan home. From there, she can see the front door, a double-width whitewashed timber door with a large pewter handle. It is standing open, the angle untouched since she got home and ran through it, calling for her child. Despite the winter wind that blows in, chilling them all, she won't allow anyone to close it.

Her eyes keep darting from the door to Shelby and back again, because surely Millie will walk in any moment. She's a clever little girl. She leads her parents around the neighbourhood on their regular Sunday walk: 'And now we go down here and then we see the doggie with the spot on his bum and then we turn up here, come on, Mum, we have to get to the kitty house quickly or he won't be there.' She would know how to return if she had, for some bizarre reason, taken herself for a walk. Has she gone on a walk? Has she run away? Has something else, something terrible happened to her? Leslie shakes her head, glances at the door again. They live in a safe neighbourhood.

Anyone seeing a child out alone would stop and ask questions, would maybe even call the police. The street is usually very quiet, with most residents parking their cars in garages behind high front gates, but Leslie has seen people around, regular dog walkers who nod at each other and at her family when they are out. Surely someone must have seen something? But then where is she? Where is her child? She has a vision of a shrouded figure in a beat-up old van stopping next to a casually strolling Millie, offering something irresistible to tempt her into the vehicle, and she feels her hand creep up to her head again. The burning sting of a few strands coming out together helps her dismiss the images. The shadowy figure in the van, kidnapping children off the street, is something conjured up in the minds of writers and filmmakers, she knows, not something that really happens. But then what *has* happened?

The queues were long at the grocery store, too long, especially since she had not gone straight to the store. 'I just need to get some food, Shelby,' she had implored only hours earlier, when she had assumed that it was an ordinary Saturday. An ordinary Saturday when she was stuck at home with her daughter and her stepdaughter while Randall played golf with potential clients or puttered around the garden or did any of the other hundred things he liked to do on a Saturday, none of which included spending time with the family.

'I'm exhausted from work, Les,' he always said, if he didn't have to be out with clients.

'I understand, but I work too and it would be nice, especially when Shelby is here, if we could go out as a family and do something.' She had an idea in her head of the four of them creating the kind of family unit she had longed for growing up as an only child. She was thirty-nine and didn't think she would have another baby, but she hoped that at some point, Shelby would start to feel like her own. From the day she first met her, she had made an effort to get to know her stepdaughter, to understand and even love her. But Shelby has always been prickly, and a lot of the time when they speak, Leslie can almost hear Bianca's voice in the girl's head, cautioning her not to get too close to her stepmother.

Shelby loves her mother and resents Leslie and sometimes, by extension, Millie. At least that's what Leslie thinks. The last weekend they spent together, Millie had been showing Shelby her new computer and Shelby had said, 'Not many three-year-olds have a computer like that. I never did when I was three.' Leslie knew those words had come straight from Bianca, who she could imagine thought Millie spoiled, but Shelby was spoiled as much by Randall. He always made sure of that.

'The world is different now,' Leslie had said, feeling, as she always did, judged by her stepdaughter.

'She likes you, Les, I promise,' Randall says to her whenever she tells him that she worries about their relationship. 'It's just hard for her to get too close because Bianca is... well, you know.'

Leslie does know. Millie, of course, adores Shelby. Her eyes light up whenever her big sister enters a room. She is more excited to see her than she is about anything else, and Shelby is actually good with her when she wants to be, patient and kind and able to tolerate hearing the same things again and again. Leslie keeps reminding herself of this. Shelby reads stories to Millie and paints her nails and watches children's television shows with her while they both munch on popcorn. She loves her little sister. But sometimes she has no desire to spend time with her. That's normal. It's normal and doesn't have to mean anything, except... where *is* Millie?

Today Shelby had not wanted to spend time with her little sister.

'Why can't you take Millie?' she had protested earlier on. 'Why? It's my Saturday too and I want to go out with Kiera. Her mum said she would drive us to the shops so we could go and look at earrings.'

'I know, but Millie makes everything take longer.'

'I do not,' came her daughter's indignant voice. 'I like the store. I can get a treat and I can talk to all the ladies and the mens who is shopping.'

'Who *are* shopping,' corrected Leslie. 'I just need to get in and out quickly, baby. Please, Shelby, I'll rush.' Even as she said the words, she knew she was lying, and she wondered if Shelby could read that in the slight flush of her cheeks. She was over-dressed for grocery shopping, with make-up and heels.

'Fine, whatever, but you better be quick.' Shelby had scowled, and Leslie had bitten down on her lip, not wanting to reprimand her for her rudeness when she needed a favour from her.

If she had gone straight to the shops, she would have only taken an hour and then maybe... She glances at the door again as Shelby speaks to the constable.

'...And I really needed to... go to the bathroom, so I just went upstairs and she was playing at her table, drawing and stuff, and then when I came downstairs, she was gone and the front door was open. I ran around the house calling her and I even went out the front and up the street, but she was just... gone,' she finishes, and as she does, her mother, Bianca, sails through the front door, her face set, her body tense, and Leslie knows she is ready for a fight.

Randall is right next to his daughter, close enough to touch her, though every time he does, Shelby shrugs him off. As he sees his ex-wife, he starts to rise from the sofa, and Leslie swallows her usual irritation at how apologetic he always seems in front of her.

'Exactly why are the police talking to our daughter without me here?' Bianca asks him.

'She's just telling them what happened,' explains Leslie. Bianca has not greeted her, has not even looked at her.

She is an imposing woman, tall and large, and seems, to Leslie, fully in control of every aspect of her life, except Randall. She lost the right to control Randall seven years ago.

Now, as she looks around the room, Leslie feels herself shrink so she is even smaller. If she had just gone straight to the shops, none of this would have happened, she is sure. And she also knows that it probably won't be long until she is found out, and then the blame for this, for her missing little girl, will fall squarely on her shoulders, and she will crumble under the weight of it, just crumble.

She had never really desired marriage and, although she wanted a child, she feared having one, because she knew that you loved a child with everything you had, and she also knew that every time she'd felt that way about someone in her life, she'd lost them. Her father had died when she was twelve – far away from her, but she was still at an age where she was clinging to the idea that he loved her and that one day they would be close. Her grandmother and grandfather had followed only a few years later. She thought she was done losing people when she married Randall and had Millie but she was wrong. Her mother had died just after Millie was born, a loss that Leslie cannot comprehend when she thinks about it.

'I'm popping to the shops for some cheese,' her mother had said when she called late one Thursday afternoon. 'Do you need anything? I'll come in after and have a cuddle with my baby.' She always referred to Millie as her baby, something that made Leslie smile every time she said it. She was deeply grateful that she had her mother to share Millie with. Even Randall wasn't as fascinated by her as she and her mother were. 'Great timing,' she had replied. 'I'm making stew for dinner and I forgot potatoes; can you pick me up a bag of baby ones?'

'Righto, see you soon,' her mother had said, and Leslie heard the clicking sound that meant she had taken off her purple-rimmed glasses and folded them up into their case so she could put on a different pair to drive. She knew her mother would be dressed in a velour tracksuit, having long ago decided that comfortable clothes were the only option for her.

After an hour and a half, Leslie was irritated. The stew needed to cook for some time or it wouldn't be tender. She called her mother's mobile phone, but she didn't answer. After another half an hour, she was worried, and she handed six-month-old Millie to Randall and drove to her mother's house, where not a single light burned. She drove home again, worry pricking at her. It was unusual for her mother not to answer her phone, not to be home at night.

Another hour passed before her phone buzzed with an unfamiliar number that turned out to be the hospital. Her mother had suffered a massive heart attack in the parking lot of the grocery store. She had been found slumped over her steering wheel by the young man who was collecting the abandoned trolleys from around the lot.

When Leslie finally got around to unloading her mother's car to sell it, weeks after the funeral, she found, among other things, the bag of baby potatoes, mouldy and sprouting. She cried until she couldn't breathe properly.

After her mother had died, Leslie understood that she was alone in the world except for Randall and Millie, and for a few months she had become hyper-vigilant, begging Randall to visit the doctor for regular check-ups and taking Millie to the hospital emergency room for every tiny spike in temperature. She didn't think she would survive losing someone else she loved.

And yet here she is now. She cannot hold on to those she loves. Her baby girl is missing and it's her fault. How can it be anyone's fault but hers?

'Well, I'm here now,' says Bianca imperiously, sitting down next to her daughter and putting her arm around her. 'You can continue.'

Leslie watches the three of them on the sofa: Randall, Bianca and Shelby. They look like a family, Shelby so obviously a combination of both her parents. Only a few hours ago, Leslie and Randall and Millie were a family. She has no idea what she is now. No idea at all.

A sob rises inside her as she imagines her daughter calling for her, and she holds her hand in front of her mouth, swallowing her pain.

'I need to go look for her,' she says, her voice breaking, tears on her cheeks.

The constable turns in his chair again. 'Not now,' he says kindly. 'Not just now.'

CHAPTER FIVE

SHELBY

Shelby doesn't like the way the old policeman is looking at her, like he can see the truth in her eyes. He can see it and any moment he's going to say, 'Right, we know what happened and we need to take you into the police station and charge you.'

'Can I go to the bathroom?' she says to her mother, because her bladder suddenly feels like it's going to burst, the same way it feels just before exams. At school, the boys are always doing stupid stuff in front of her to get her attention, but when it comes to exams, she feels like the dumbest person in the world. She's at the top of most of her classes, but that doesn't help, because every exam is a chance to prove to everyone that she's an idiot and a failure.

Well, she *was* at the top of her classes. In the last month she's failed two exams and she's gotten three detentions. Her mother keeps asking, 'What on earth is wrong with you?' and her father says, 'Is something bothering you?' and she's noticed that they are really interested now that she's messing up. If someone had told her when she was six years old that one day her parents would not be interested in her, she would have laughed. At six she was the centre of both their universes, at seven she realised they had complicated lives of their own, and now she knows they have very little interest in her at all. Unless she's stuffing things up – and she's doing a really good job of that now.

Her mother is busy on her phone, texting her stepfather no doubt. If someone had to line the two of them, Shelby and Trevor, up next to each other and say, 'One of them has to die,' Shelby is pretty sure her mother would hesitate before saving her daughter. Maybe that's being dramatic, but it feels that way sometimes. 'Not everything has to be about you, Shelby' is her mother's current favourite line, but Shelby wonders if anything, anything at all, is ever about her any more.

'Of course, of course you can, sweetheart,' says her dad, answering for her mother, who probably didn't even hear her ask, and he squeezes her shoulder, forcing her to shrug him off.

She stands up from the sofa and runs upstairs to the bathroom that is attached to her room, needing to be far away from all of them. It's decorated in cool brown and cream marble tiles and it has a huge bathtub and a vanity unit with a mirrored cupboard that's big enough for all her make-up. The bathroom is just for her, and she loves it – has loved it from the moment Leslie told her it was hers for when she came to stay – but she also hates it because Leslie is not her mother and this should have been the house she lived in with her mother and her father, not her stepmother. Then everything would have been okay; well, not totally okay, because she would still be suffering through each day at school, but better.

Her parents got divorced when she was five, or at least that was when her mother said to her father one night, 'I've had enough, Randall. You're not interested in anything except that stupid software that's never going to sell. Give it up or let me get on with my life.' Shelby was supposed to be asleep, but she was awake and listening to her parents fight. She had been doing that in the months leading up to them separating. When she thinks back on that time, she knows that at some point their arguments went from just being boring old married-people arguments about taking out the garbage and making a mess in the kitchen to something stranger. That was when she started listening in on them. After the divorce, both her parents assured her that they loved her and she got used to going between her dad's apartment and her mum's apartment and having to remember all the stuff she needed. There were different rules at each place, but that kind of worked to her advantage. It was nice to have some time away from her mum and her need for her to be in bed or playing quietly or just out of the way. Her dad didn't mind if she stayed up late and he let her eat what she wanted, and even though he was always busy working, he still seemed happy to see her. She thought everything would be okay, but then it all changed.

She will never get used to how angry her mum is about everything, especially after her dad actually found someone to invest millions of dollars in his software and built a big company when she was six. And then he met and married Leslie, and that made her mum so angry she threw a mug against a wall in the kitchen and it shattered, the pieces going everywhere. Shelby remembers being scared of her that night. Her mum didn't seem like her mum at all. 'After everything he put me through, what am I left with? Nothing, that's what, nothing,' she had screamed. She wasn't screaming at Shelby – more at the whole world – but Shelby felt sad anyway, because her mum still had her and she wasn't nothing.

In the bathroom, she uses the toilet and then she stands in front of the mirror for a long time, washing her hands, letting the warm water comfort her. She meets her eyes in the mirror and she doesn't like what she sees there. 'What have you done?'

she whispers to herself. 'What have you done?' Leaving the water running, she pulls her phone out of her pocket and thinks about texting Kiera, but then she doesn't. Instead, she reads back through all the messages between them and feels a shiver run through her body. What if they check her phone? Police always do that, don't they?

Sorry can't come my stepmother is forcing me to babysit.

OMG she always does that. It's not fair that you have to spend Saturday afternoon with your bratty little sister.

I know and it always happens like this. It's so annoying.

Yeah, it's easier being an only child, that's for sure.

I know. I wish I still was!!!!

Her fingers move over the texts, and then quickly, before anyone can come looking for her, she deletes them. They won't speak to Kiera. Unless they do. Inside her chest, her heart beats faster. What if they go and ask Kiera for her phone?

'They won't,' she reassures her reflection. She's not going to tell them Kiera was here and there's no way Kiera will tell anyone. Kiera is good at keeping secrets, especially ones that could affect her.

She picks up her brush with the wooden handle and starts brushing her hair in long, soft strokes while she looks at her reflection. Brushing her hair always calms her down. Her mother used to do it for her, even when she got too old for it, but she doesn't any more. Her mother is pretty much obsessed with Trevor, and sometimes Shelby can see her looking at her like she can't wait for her to grow up and move out and leave the two of them alone. Shelby can't wait to grow up either, to live on her own, leave school and be in control of her life and who is allowed to be in it.

Millie has only been in her life for three years, but in those three years she has changed everything. Shelby went from being the first person her dad looked at to the second person, and sometimes he doesn't even look at her at all. No one can compete with a baby and a toddler, no matter how clever and pretty they are. Her mother doesn't really want her in her house and her father is only interested in his new child, and Shelby is… nothing. Her mother was right all those years ago.

She wipes a tear from her cheek. She wishes she could just tell everyone the truth, but it's more complicated than her just confessing. What would jail be like? She shudders. She can't go to jail. She has to keep lying.

When it happened, she had known that Leslie would be home soon and she knew that there was no way to keep her missing little sister a secret, and so she had called her, after she opened the front door wide, called her and cried that Millie was missing.

She picks up her phone again, staring at the picture of her and Kiera. Kiera is her first real best friend, in the way that best friends seem in movies. Kiera and her mother only moved here a few months ago. She's never had a father. Her mother got pregnant from a sperm donor, something that Kiera told her on the first night they had a sleepover. 'Gross,' Shelby had giggled, and Kiera had laughed along with her. 'I know, right, really gross, but she really wanted a baby.'

'Do you miss having a father?' Shelby had asked as she popped all the brown M&Ms in her mouth.

'I don't know. You have a father and a stepfather. What's that like?' Kiera ate all the other M&Ms, cramming them into her mouth in a jumble of colours. Shelby shrugged, because she didn't know how to talk about that stuff except to say that her parents were driving her crazy.

She didn't want to make having two fathers sound bad – she wanted Kiera to envy her, just a little, because there was a lot she envied about Kiera. Like how she wasn't scared to tell other kids or teachers or even the principal what she thought, like how she was the fastest runner in the school, like how she didn't care about anyone else's opinion of her. Kiera made life seem easy, but for Shelby it was complicated and messy and made her mostly sad.

Millie only has one father, Shelby's father, and sometimes when Shelby watches the two of them doing a puzzle together, both so quiet and thoughtful, she wonders if he ever spent the same kind of time with her. She doesn't think so. But maybe it's because when she was little, he was always working on his software thing and now he's the head of a company and he's very, very rich. Or maybe it's because he loves Millie more than he loves Shelby, because everyone loves Millie. Shelby calls her Millie Billy, and her father and Leslie call her Millie Molly after some character in a children's book that Leslie loved.

Shelby bends forward and cups her hands under the running water, pushing the tap to cold and waiting for it to cool down. She drinks deeply, her mouth dry. She has no idea how she's going to fix this. The loss of her little sister doesn't feel real, but she knows she's gone. She saw it with her own eyes. She wants to cry, but there is a dead feeling inside her, as though the Shelby who feels things is also gone.

'Shelby,' she hears her father call from downstairs, and she knows she can't hide in the bathroom any more. She opens the door and walks into the passage. Millie's room is right next to the bathroom, and the door is open. Everything is pink in Millie's room, from the carpet to the curtains to the duvet and blanket on the bed. She has left her pyjamas on the floor, and Shelby steps inside, inhaling her sister's unique fruity smell, and picks them up. She folds them and places them under her pillow.

'Goodnight, Millie Billy,' she whispers. 'Goodbye.'

And then she holds her breath so she doesn't open her mouth and scream and scream because her chest hurts and her eyes are burning and her life as she knew it is over.

CHAPTER SIX

RUTH

In the kitchen, I slice up a tangy red apple, placing the slices in a perfect circle, and then I cut wafer-thin slices of sharp cheddar cheese, laying those on top of the apple. Rice crackers are the final addition to the perfect late lunch, exactly ten rice crackers and ten slices of apple and ten slices of cheese. I sit in front of the television watching a soap opera I like as I wait for the news. I enjoy the depictions of beautiful homes filled with beautiful but horribly troubled people who take time to think before they speak. The storyline is easy to dip in and out of, so it's soothing to watch.

I have eaten the same lunch every day for the last ten years. I usually eat at exactly 1 p.m., but today I was busy at that time, and then everything took longer than I thought it would because of... what I saw. Still, even though it's late, I need to have my lunch or the day won't feel right. It's not right, far from it, but I must take charge of what I can take charge of, and lunch is easy enough.

I am a creature of habit. I didn't used to be. Before... before everything, I was a normal thirteen-year-old child with curly brown hair and freckles, a gap between my oversized front teeth. In the mirror now, which I mostly avoid, my hair is still brown and curly, still long, and there is still a gap between my front teeth, but smaller now. I am very strict about oral hygiene, brushing and flossing twice a day. I haven't been to a dentist since my mother and I moved into this house and I refused to leave. I refused to leave to go to school, to go to the store, to go to the dentist.

'No,' I said, whenever she asked me to go somewhere with her. 'No.' I didn't argue, because she would have been able to deal with that. She would have argued back, yelled and shouted, but there was nothing she could do if I simply refused. One of my mother's strengths was her ability to get you to see her side of things, but if you didn't listen to what she had to say, there wasn't much she could do. The day we moved into this house, into my grandmother's house, I felt I was finally safe. I needed to create my piles to make sure I stayed safe, but I understood that leaving the house, walking out the door and into the world, made me unsafe, and everything that had happened could potentially happen again. And so I stayed inside, surrounded by my stacks, safe from everything and everyone.

The only thing I did readily agree to do was learn to drive. My mother taught me in the yellow Beetle, and even though I had to knock down and restack quite a few different collections before I got into the car each time, I knew that I was safe in there with the doors locked and the tinted windows up, shielded from the world. Now it's my moving safe space and getting into it is easy. Getting out of it once I reach my destination is something else altogether, but I keep trying. Many weeks go by when all I do is take the car around the block to make sure it's in good working order. But sometimes I stop at a park or by the beach and step out, resting my hand on the bonnet as I admire a different view to my small garden. I stand there for as long as I can until the adrenaline rises up inside me, forcing me to flee, to return to my collections.

We went to a lot of therapy, my mother and I. Or therapy came to us. We went together and we went apart and still no one could help me overcome my fear of going outside, where other people were, of being in the world.

'Can you tell me when Ruth started to develop a fear of going out?' a therapist named Beth Hawley asked my mother. I saw Beth when I was seventeen. She had long grey hair she wound into a bun, and she always arrived late and flustered from another appointment.

'No,' said my mother, her head shaking quickly. She had really thought about this but she couldn't find the answer. I believe she knew. She had seen, had realised, but she thought it was just a blip, something small, and that I had moved on – *she* certainly had.

My mother, Beth and I were sitting on the sofa in our living room, which had been tidied and cleaned for the visit. On the elegantly carved, delicate timber coffee table a silver pot of tea sat next to some thin white china cups, all of it belonging to my grandmother, who was in her room at the time, sleeping away her day. At least at my grandmother's house I was prepared to leave my room. In our old house, in a dead-end road on a tiny piece of land, I had retreated from the world to my room, and there I stayed until we moved in with my grandmother when I was sixteen.

I moved schools at twelve and went from my small, safe primary school into a large, sprawling high school filled with over a thousand students. I was immediately lost and confused and lonely, but eventually I settled in and made friends, and I would have had a perfectly reasonable life if not for what happened when I was thirteen, fourteen, fifteen. My self-imposed separation from the world might have started with the slight panic I felt every morning at having to attend school, but I had no idea what was coming. No idea at all.

I've had a lot of therapy. But the thing about that is, if you're not ready to change, it doesn't work. If you are not committed to helping yourself, if you cannot reveal your terrible secrets, it's basically useless.

After we moved back in with my grandmother, it was okay to be out of my room as long I had quick access to a pile of things I could knock over and rearrange if the doorbell rang or someone called or a panic attack reared up out of nowhere when I was watching television.

What is wrong with you? What is wrong with you? What is wrong with you? lamented my mother.

'Leave her be, Nora,' my grandmother, whose name was Eleanor, always said to my mother when she despaired. She knew the value of collecting things, and now I wonder if that was because she herself was a collector, or because she understood what I was trying to do. It was never overtly discussed; no one ever said, 'What exactly are you hiding from, Ruth?' or, the more pertinent question, '*Who* are you hiding from, Ruth?' Every few months, my mother asked me what was wrong, what was troubling me, why I behaved the way I did, but I knew her questions were designed to give me the freedom to not answer. Sometimes people don't actually want the answers. When someone walks past an acquaintance in the street and says, 'Hey, how are you?' they have no desire to hear anything beyond 'Fine, thanks, and you?' My mother was desperate for me to be 'fine, thanks'.

She did her best, but to do better than that would have required her to sacrifice herself and her needs, and she couldn't do that. My grandmother's house, now my house, is a safe space. I feel her spirit here, watching over me, protecting me, just like I do in her car.

During an advert break, I check my bank balance, something I do two or three times a day. When she died, my mother left me a small inheritance and this house. She worked in retail – between husbands and when she finally gave up on the husband idea – and she was quite good at it. She sold everything from clothing to cars. I have enough to get by. I don't need much.

Since my mother died, six months ago, something has released inside me – or perhaps I have released myself from everything I was keeping from her – and I have begun to venture out. I had to, of course. There was no one to bring me things to add to my collections. Even before she died, I had started roaming the streets at night, especially on recycling day, gloved hands at the ready. Getting older had helped me feel more able to deal with whatever came my way. That and the small pocket knife I carried, which looks harmless enough but, at the touch of a button, produces a blade large enough to do damage, sharp enough to cause pain.

Since my mother died, I have begun forcing myself to venture out during the day, not just to drive somewhere and admire a view, but to actually interact with the world, the unsafe, uncertain, chaotic world. I tell myself, *You can do this*. I am afraid that one day I will really need to leave the house and simply be unable to do so. I fear dying alone in here because I'm too scared to get help. My back tooth hurts sometimes and I worry that I have a cavity. It may be possible to avoid the doctor and the dentist forever, especially with the internet and its endless advice, but perhaps one day there will be no alternative. So I am preparing, training the way a soldier does, readying myself for hours and days outside, with small missions.

Before I leave the house, I add layers to my body. I start with a singlet, pull on a thin top and a jumper on top of that and then finish with a puffer jacket. I wear sunglasses and a cap as well. It will be harder in summer, but I have no idea where I will be in the summer, no idea how this is all going to play out.

After today, after the last couple of weeks, I wish I hadn't ever forced myself out. I knew what was out there, but I didn't know it was waiting for me.

I hate that I've had to leave during the day as much as I have, but it has been necessary.

The news comes on and the smart woman newsreader with her neat blonde bob and deep velvet voice says, 'A child has been reported missing from her home this afternoon. Millie Everleigh is three years old, with black hair and blue eyes.' A picture flashes onto the screen and I almost choke, a mouthful of food refusing to go down. I spit it out and wipe my mouth with the back of my hand, my appetite gone. 'We will now cross to the Everleigh house, where Millie's parents are waiting to make an appeal to the public for information...'

I turn off the television quickly. I can't see. I can't.

They are looking for her already. But of course they would be. They're looking but they won't find her. I know that.

CHAPTER SEVEN

LESLIE

3.30 p.m.

She and Randall stand in front of the reporters who are grouped on their front lawn, one or two, she notices, standing in the flower bed. She can see already that the small rose bushes, just beginning to bud, will not survive being trampled on. At this thought her eyes well up and she is forced to brush away her tears, blinking quickly and sniffing as she wishes she had a tissue. There are a lot of people here, all of them straining forward, iPhones and cameras and microphones pointed towards Leslie and Randall.

An amber alert will only be issued if the police feel that Millie has been abducted rather than just wandered off. 'And when exactly do you make that decision?' Randall asked the constable.

'After the press conference we'll give it some more time to find out if anyone has seen her, and then we'll rethink.'

'But why not just do it now? Why wait?' Leslie questioned him, frustrated at the idea that not everything that could be done was being done.

'We have procedures and rules in place for a reason,' the constable replied, kindly. Leslie can hear in the way he speaks – in the way he listens and reacts – that he has been dealing with people on the worst days of their lives for a very long time. He doesn't promise anything, probably knowing that he can never do that, and he doesn't get upset when voices are raised and tears begin falling. He is calm and speaks quietly and Leslie wonders if he is the same way at home with his family, or if he changes when he is out of the public eye.

The neighbourhood has been searched and Millie has been gone for around two hours, according to the time Shelby gave the police. Such a short amount of time, but it feels like a lifetime.

'Right, so you looked for her for quite a while before you called your stepmother,' the constable had stated when Shelby explained that she had gone up to the bathroom just after 1 p.m. No need to ask how she knew the time; her gaze is always firmly focused on her phone.

'Um, yeah, yes... I thought she was playing,' Shelby had replied. 'And then when I couldn't find her, I looked again and I went outside and then I... I called Leslie.'

Millie is terrible at hide-and-seek. She is easily bored and will call out 'come find me already' after only a few minutes if she has not been located. She also hides in places like behind the sofa or her bedroom door. She likes the excitement of being found rather than the secrecy of hiding. Shelby knows this, and for a moment, listening to her speak to the constable, Leslie fixed her gaze on her stepdaughter's face, desperate to ask why she was lying, but then she had looked away. Maybe Millie was different when Leslie wasn't there. Maybe she enjoyed playing hide-and-seek with Shelby more than she did with Leslie. But perhaps, just perhaps, Shelby was lying.

Leslie watches an earnest discussion between a cameraman and a reporter with a slash of maroon lipstick across her lips about where to film, and she wishes she had thought to at least add some blush to her cheeks. She's going to look like a ghoul on television.

Millie has been gone for over two hours and that's the only thing that matters. The first twenty-four hours – that number that is always quoted in missing persons or missing children cases as being the timescale that matters – is ticking away. 'Most missing children are found within the first twenty-four hours,' Constable Willow told her as they waited for the reporters to arrive, for the people who would help spread the word to race over to their house, thirsty for a story on a quiet Saturday afternoon.

Twenty-two hours to go? Twenty-one and a half hours to go? Each minute is important, each sixty seconds bringing her daughter closer to home or leading her further away.

Leslie feels herself stepping back, away from the lights that keep flashing and the enquiring faces. Randall rests his hand on her back, pushing her forward again, preventing her from escaping.

'Can't you do this?' she whispers.

'It needs to be both of us,' he whispers back. 'If someone has her...' He doesn't finish the sentence. *No one has her, she just wandered off. She's going to be found soon, soon, soon.*

Randall's face is pale, and she reads exhaustion in the bags under his eyes. In the last few weeks, he hasn't slept well. He tosses and turns all night, and a few days ago, in desperate need of a full night's sleep, she asked him to move into the guest bedroom. He hadn't argued, only nodded his head. 'I'm sorry, Les,' he had said. Bianca has been on his mind a lot. His ex-wife calls him almost daily to discuss Shelby's issues, and from what he has told Leslie, it seems Bianca is certain that Shelby's behaviour is worse after she returns from their house.

'She wants us to take a break from seeing her,' he'd said only last night. 'She says Shelby is always more difficult when she's had a weekend here. She says she sends her to us happy and calm and she comes back filled with anger and aggression.'

'That's ridiculous,' said Leslie. 'She's your child. Bianca has no right to stop you seeing her. Shelby is as happy here as she is at home. I mean, she's... Maybe it's just her age.'

'Maybe, but she won't talk to me.' He had pushed a finger behind his glasses and rubbed at his eye, and then he had looked away from her. She understood then that he was truly worried that Bianca had enough power to deny him access to his child. 'Maybe Bianca's right. I mean... I don't know how to deal with a twelve-year-old girl,' he said turning back to look at her. Bianca's words, so obviously Bianca's cruel words.

Teachers from Shelby's school have begun complaining, sending home emails about her performance in class, about her attitude, about her general behaviour. Something is wrong, but Shelby won't tell anyone what it is. 'I hate school' is as close as she has gotten to communicating why her behaviour has suddenly changed.

Randall had been disbelieving. 'But you used to love school. You love English and history. Who's your history teacher again? Mr Jordan – you said he made everything feel like it happened only yesterday, made it interesting and exciting,' he had protested.

'I don't want to talk about it,' Shelby said, shutting down the conversation as she pushed her food around her dinner plate.

No one, it seemed, quite knew how to deal with her.

Leslie reflects that this conversation only happened two weeks ago. Two weeks ago, Shelby was struggling at school and uncommunicative, and now they are here. Surely it's all connected? But she can't exactly tell the police that Shelby hates school and that's why her half-sister is missing. It's a long bow to draw.

Privately Leslie feels that Randall is a little afraid of what Shelby might say if she really opened up to him. He's different with Millie, but then Millie is still so little and she has no idea what he would have been like with Shelby at that age. If he would give her permission, she would try to talk to Shelby, but he is wary of upsetting Bianca, who seems determined to make sure that Shelby sees Leslie as a Stepmother with a capital S. Leslie would like it to be different, and she knows that Randall would love to come home to a house that felt cohesive and peaceful as much as she would.

'Can you get out of the flower beds?' she wants to shout at all the people who are standing in her front yard, but she would look crazy. She wishes this thing would start so that it could be over and she can have some time with Randall and Shelby to try and work out what might have happened. No, not work out what might have happened – so they can have some time to get Shelby to tell the truth.

How can she be thinking like this? She's a terrible person.

Randall keeps pushing his shoulders back, standing up taller and straighter as lights flash when their pictures are taken – the couple with the missing child. She imagines a million televisions and internet sites, many millions of eyes, many millions of ears, all listening, all willing to look.

She'll be found. She has to be found.

'Get on with it,' mutters Randall quietly, and she can see he's holding on as tightly as she is. They are not the kind of parents who lose their child – but then what kind of parents are they?

She'd met Randall at the advertising agency where she was head of graphic design.

It was not love at first sight. He was too tall and skinny, too awkward and ten years older than she was, at forty-four. He needed a new logo and a social media package for the software he had spent years developing. He had finally secured funding from a huge company in America and she could tell that he didn't quite know what to do with all the money he now had, as he went about setting up a business. He learned quickly, though, and to look at him now, as he dons an expensive suit and goes to speak to more investors, no one would know that he used to feel sick to his stomach about meeting new clients. Ageing has made him distinguished, with greying hair, and his body is lean and fit, different to a lot of men, who gain weight and go bald.

At their first meeting, he later told her, he had been nervous because he thought her beautiful, and while Leslie had dealt with her fair share of male attention, she had never been considered beautiful. Pretty, delicate and fragile were the words that most men used as they attempted to rescue her from the world. Randall was interested in her work, in the way she thought, in her eye for design. Nerves made him confess more than he should have to a woman he was speaking to for business purposes.

'My wife hated that I spent all my free hours working on it. She told me that it would never amount to anything. But I couldn't give up,' he told her as he shared everything the software could do for businesses big and small. He was so proud, and his enthusiasm was so infectious that she found herself working just a little harder for him, wanting him to be happy with what she came up with. Over long lunches and afternoons in the office, because he insisted on coming in to see her even though everything could be done by email or on the phone, she found herself falling for him. He made her laugh and he was delighted by everything, interested in everything. He was exciting to be around.

Meeting Shelby had been hard. She had been unsure of what to do with a seven-year-old child who was still hoping that her parents would get back together. She could sense Bianca's resentment at Randall's success only happening after the divorce in the things her stepdaughter said.

'My mum never got to have a big house like this one,' Shelby
told her when they bought the house.

'My mum doesn't have dresses that are that nice,' she said
on looking through Leslie's closet.

Randall was generous with child support even though he
didn't have to give Bianca so much, but money was never very
important to him. His work was what he was passionate about.
His work and his children. He loved Shelby and Millie desperately. Leslie has real, deep love for her stepdaughter, she knows
that about herself, but Shelby has never made their relationship
easy. Leslie feels like she has to work for every smile, every
moment of happiness. But she tries to limit her complaints to
Randall about this, only going to him when she is desperate for
his reassurance that Shelby doesn't actually hate her. Shelby
was part of the package and she never wanted to come between
them. Lately, though, Shelby has even been turning on Randall.

And now they are here and Leslie's child is missing. Her
child. Her only child, because one was all she was ever going to
have.

'If I could have your attention, please... Thanks, everyone,'
says Constable Dickerson, holding up his hands to the assem-
bled throng, waiting for them to grow quiet. 'We are appealing
for public help in finding Millie Everleigh. That's M-I-L-L-I-E
E-V-E-R-L-E-I-G-H. She is three years old, ninety-five centime-
tres tall and approximately fourteen kilos. She has blue eyes and
long black hair. She is wearing pink corduroy dungarees with a
blue long-sleeve top underneath and pink Ugg boots. It is
believed she left home at around one fifteen p.m. We are asking
all members of the public to be on the lookout for this child.
Searches are ongoing in the neighbourhood and we have a
group in Wonderland Park, which is a twenty-minute walk
from here. Anyone who is in the park and watching this is asked
to keep an eye out...'

At the mention of the large park near their house, Leslie

feels her stomach turn over. It was the first place she had suggested to the police. Millie loves the park, with its man-made lakes filled with ducks and its playground with two climbing frames and two different swing sets next to a cubby house. The lakes, filled with cold, still water, have always frightened Leslie, and when she and Millie are there, feeding the ducks, she always has one hand on her little girl. Millie is learning to swim, but she cannot swim properly, not yet. Randall was going to search the park, but it was too big for him to cover alone and the police were on their way by then. She knows that if they don't find Millie soon, they will begin exploring the lakes, police divers in their wetsuits swimming through the murky water looking for the body of her child. *No, no, please no.*

Constable Dickerson turns towards them, saying, 'And now Millie's mother and father would like to…' He steps back and gestures at her and Randall, and together they move forward, closer to the lights and the questions.

As Randall begins his appeal for people to help find Millie, Leslie sees herself pulling out of the driveway at 11.45 this morning, knowing that she would not be back in an hour, knowing that she had something else to do before the shopping, knowing that she was keeping this information from Shelby and from Randall. When she was little, her grandmother – her father's mother – had always said, her bony finger wagging in Leslie's face, 'A secret kept is a secret you live to regret.' As a child, Leslie's secrets had been minor indiscretions, like taking an extra cookie, not brushing her teeth, or staying up past her bedtime, reading under the covers. As a teenager, secrets were delicious bits of information, traded with only the closest of friends, things that were deemed to be of great importance one day but faded into insignificance the next. As an adult, secrets in a marriage are sometimes necessary, but Leslie has never seen the need for them until today, and she thought she would have time to tell Randall, to explain. But it's too late for that now and she cannot see how to engineer some time alone with Randall with so many people around them, so many scrutinising faces.

She watches her husband's mouth move as she tries to look the way people will imagine the mother of a missing child should look. But she's sure she's getting it wrong. *A secret kept is a secret you live to regret.* As a child, that regret had manifested in the form of small punishments: no ice cream after dinner, no television time. But what is the cost of secrets as an adult? Surely, surely this is too high a price.

In the crowd of journalists, she notices one man staring directly at her. He doesn't even seem to be concentrating on the press conference, only watching her, and she knows... she can feel that she is doing this incorrectly. She doesn't look right; she doesn't look the way they need her to look. The tweets and comments will be amassing on social media as Randall speaks. She can just imagine them.

Why does she look so calm?

Being rich doesn't keep your kids safe.

Why was the stepdaughter left with the child? Twelve is too young to babysit.

What was the mother doing all that time? Something fishy about this if you ask me.

Children don't just disappear.

They will turn on her first; all those who react with sympathy when they hear a child is missing will eventually turn on her.

It's what happens every time. Leslie has watched press conferences like these and felt herself judging the mother of the missing child. *How could you have let that happen? Weren't you watching your little boy, your little girl?* But *she* has let it happen. She handed the care of her child over to a twelve-year-old obviously going through some issues, and waltzed out the door.

Shelby has only begun babysitting Millie since she turned

twelve. Leslie had looked up the legal age for babysitting in Australia, needing to be sure she was making the right decision, only to find that there is no actual law. But a person under eighteen cannot be held legally responsible for what happens to your child, so you have to ensure they are mature enough to be in charge. She and Randall had discussed this together and with Shelby, and there had been many conversations about what to do in the event of an emergency. There is a list on the fridge for the police and the doctor and even the neighbours. Shelby had declared herself ready and so far it had gone really well, the girls enjoying time alone together.

Shelby is mature enough to babysit Millie, clever enough to know what to do if something happens and level-headed enough not to panic for no reason.

But perhaps today she had no desire to be any of that, and no desire to take care of Millie at all. Today Shelby was not capable because today Shelby didn't want to, and that should have been enough for Leslie to take Millie with her to the grocery store. It should have been enough. But Leslie wasn't only going to the grocery store.

The press throng begin shouting questions, and Leslie feels herself moving away. They are going to turn on her. She will answer a question incorrectly or she will not look sad enough or she will simply open her mouth and scream her fear and they will turn on her. And they're right to, they should.

She moves further and further back until there is only Randall standing next to the constable trying to answer the questions that are thrown out, fly-fishing for any possible reaction.

You stated that another child was babysitting her. Are the children often left alone?

Have the neighbours been interviewed?

Were police called immediately?

Do the police have any idea where she may have gone?

Who was the last person to see Millie?

What kind of mood was she in? Was she distressed in any way?

And then Randall moves back as well, and it is the constable who deals with them the way he deals with everyone – slowly, patiently, kindly.

Leslie looks around her front garden, despairing at gouged-out bits of grass and the destroyed flower bed. There are so many people here and she should be grateful, she knows she should be, but each of them is one more person between her and her stepchild, between her and the truth, between her and her daughter. And so she wishes they would all just leave, just go and leave them alone. But that's not going to happen, so she stands off to one side, watching them as they watch her, praying that in all the looking and all the watching, someone will see something.

CHAPTER EIGHT

SHELBY

They wouldn't let her out in front to talk to the reporters, but she has been standing by the window, watching it all happen. It feels weird to be looking out of the window, like she's some kind of crazy stalker. It all got so big so fast – a nightmare come to life. She can't believe how many people there are. Somehow they all look... not sad or sorry... they look excited, like this is the best thing to happen on a slow weekend in Sydney. They make her sick to her stomach, which is already tied up in knots and starting to hurt. In her hand, her phone vibrates and she looks down.

U better not tell anyone I was there

She drops the phone, shock and fear burning through her, and then hurriedly picks it up again, hoping no one has seen her reaction. She immediately deletes the text, like she did all the other messages between her and Kiera.

Kiera is not the kind of friend her parents would want her to have. They don't know that yet, not yet, but they must be starting to get a clue from all the emails home. Kiera's mother works a lot because it's just her, and she has all these rules in place to keep Kiera safe. Shelby knows that if it was her who had to complete a whole lot of chores and get her homework done before she was allowed computer time, then she would have done everything in the right order. But that's not who Kiera is, and the more time they spend together, the more that's not who Shelby is any more. She never would have imagined that she would be the kind of person who would leave school at lunchtime, sneaking out the back gate where there's never a teacher on duty and just running off to the shops. But that's exactly what happened on Friday. She's pretty sure her parents are going to get called about that on Monday, but yesterday, she hadn't cared. On Monday they probably won't care either. Where will she be on Monday? Who will she be?

On Friday, she and Kiera had gone to a café, flushed with success at escaping school and an afternoon of history. They couldn't stop giggling as they ordered chocolate milkshakes and a plate of chips to share. When the waitress brought their order, giving them both a sideways look, like she knew they were doing the wrong thing, Shelby laughed so hard she snorted. While they ate, they took all these crazy pictures together and everyone who followed her on Instagram had liked them and asked where they were and she had felt so brave and so strong. She hasn't felt like that lately, more like she's small and weak and not worth anyone's time, but Kiera makes her feel something else, something better. Kiera also has a bit of a mean streak. She doesn't want Shelby to have any other friends. She doesn't want Shelby to do anything with anyone else except her.

She especially doesn't like it when Millie interrupts them when they're together. When she stayed over for the first time, she didn't want to watch television with Millie before she went to bed, didn't want to sit in the room while Shelby read her sister a story, and she had been really angry when Millie woke them early the next morning. Shelby figured that was because she was an only child. But today she realised that Kiera actively disliked three-year-old Millie, and that was because she hated it when Shelby paid attention to anyone but her.

She's deleted the texts where they talk about Millie, but she'll never tell anyone what they spoke about on the call they had after Leslie left, when Millie was busy looking through all the polish colours so Shelby could paint her nails.

'Why can't you just leave her there for a bit? She's old enough,' Kiera had said.

'I can't, she's only three and my step-monster would go insane if she found out.' She always referred to Leslie as her step-monster when they talked, even though she didn't really think of her like that. Sometimes Leslie is a bit much, too emotional and too overly friendly, but Shelby knows that every time they are together, she tries really hard to keep her happy. It's weird to watch an adult trying so hard to be her friend, and it's something that almost makes her feel sorry for her step-mother. But no one else in Shelby's life cares about how she feels like Leslie does, and somehow that makes Shelby angrier at her than she is at her mother, who is acting like she's never been in a relationship before, or her father, who has made himself a new family to go with his new life of rich businessman.

'Maybe I can just come over and we can hang out,' Kiera had said on the phone.

'I don't know...' Shelby had hesitated, because Kiera has a way of suggesting they do stuff that makes it sound really exciting – like taking alcohol from the whitewashed wood cabinet in the living room, or sneaking out of the house to smoke a cigarette from the pack she stole from her mother, or taking one of the pills she calls her mother's 'happy pills' – but seem just on the edge of dangerous to Shelby. Kiera has only been over to her mother's house and her father's house when there have been adults at home, and Shelby has always been able to say 'my mother would know' or 'my father will hear'. And that's been enough to stop her, until today.

'Come on, Shelby, don't be such a baby. She's gone for an hour and we can just hang out. I'll sneak out the back door when we hear her come home.'

'But what will your mum say?'

'My mum is out shopping. I told her that if you weren't coming, I didn't want to go with her. Anyway, she has no interest in spending the day with me. This morning she told me I was ungrateful for everything she does and blah, blah, blah. You know parents.'

'How will you get here?'

'Bus. Come on, please... It's lonely here on my own.' Kiera had put on her sad voice and Shelby knew she would give in – she usually did. It wasn't like she didn't have other friends; it was more that there was something different in the way Kiera looked at her. She didn't care if Shelby aced every test or not. Susanna, who used to be her kind-of best friend, would always look shocked if she got a B on anything. And Kiera didn't seem to care that she looked the way she looked, maybe because she was so pretty herself. Shelby was used to everyone telling her how pretty she was, and she was grateful that she'd won some kind of genetic lottery, but sometimes she felt like it meant she was never allowed to look anything except perfect. Her mother thought she was dying to be a model and spend all day having people take pictures of her, but she hated that idea. She felt like she would eventually just become a picture, a two-dimensional image on a page for someone to look at and point out her flaws. And she hated it when random people told her she was pretty, like the strange man on the train when she and Leslie went shopping in the city for her birthday. 'Aren't you just lovely,' he said and Leslie put her arm around her and pulled her closer. 'Yes, she is,' she answered for Shelby, who immediately felt gross and exposed. Older men shouldn't look at young girls like that, but they did, she knew they did. She preferred selfies because she was in control of that and she got to decide who could look at her.

Kiera didn't see the pretty Shelby or the clever Shelby or Shelby the annoying daughter who was in the way. She just saw Shelby.

'Okay, come over,' she had agreed, and that was the worst thing she could have done. The very worst thing, because it was the start of this nightmare. What will Kiera do to her if she tells anyone that she was here? How angry will she be? Today, she hadn't just let her mean streak come out; today she almost became someone else, someone that Shelby should never have allowed near her little sister.

If Kiera hadn't come over, she wouldn't have yelled at Millie and Millie wouldn't have threatened to run away, and then the two of them wouldn't have had to chase her down the street after Kiera opened the door and said, 'Go on then, you little brat. Run.'

And then... then *they* wouldn't have caught her.

CHAPTER NINE

RUTH

I find myself in need of a drink, and I go back to the kitchen, where I grab a can of raspberry-flavoured diet soda out of the fridge. It's sickly sweet and tastes a little like plastic, but I gulp it down gratefully, clearing my mouth of the taste of the apple and cheese.

Back in front of the television, I take a deep breath and turn the set back on, whispering, 'You can do this, Ruth' to myself. I see that I have just missed the parents of the little girl speaking. I turn up the sound and listen to a policeman answering questions. Behind him I can see her mother, obviously her mother. She is standing apart from everyone else. There are a few men in the background as well, but I can't tell which one is her husband, the father of the missing little girl. I can't tell, but I know which one he is. I know. I just need it confirmed. I feel like I need to get closer to the screen so I can see better, but that's ridiculous. I remember my mother pulling me back from the television when I was little. 'You'll get square eyes,' she would say, and I would imagine my almond-shaped eyes turning into perfect squares. I didn't mind the idea.

I sometimes wonder if my mother is looking down on me, as

they say. Is she watching me? Can she see what my life is and does she regret anything?

It would be easy for me to dismiss her if she was simply a terrible mother, but she wasn't. She was like most people, a melding of good and bad and someone who thought – who believed – she was doing her best in a difficult situation. My father had left when I was only three, just like the little girl they are searching for. I'm not sure I really registered that he was gone for a while. He left early in the morning for work and he travelled a lot to different parts of the country, selling farming equipment. I was very used to him not being there. Only when my mother started going out at night, leaving me with our next-door neighbour's fifteen-year-old daughter, did I realise that something had changed. I was happy enough to spend my evenings with Charlene. She used to brush and braid my hair and then let me watch soap operas with her until way past my bedtime.

I was less happy when my mother started bringing home the men.

The first morning I found one of them in the kitchen, I let out a high-pitched scream, fear leading to tears. He was standing by the kettle waiting for it to boil, wearing jeans and a shirt that he had neglected to button. He was tall, filling the space, and smelled strongly of something musky.

'Shut up, Ruth,' my mother said, coming into the kitchen draped in a silk dressing gown with a cigarette between her lips, smoke wafting through the air. I closed my mouth. My mother carried some of the same musky smell with her, not her usual light rose scent.

'This is Bernie,' she told me, as she got out a cereal bowl for me and filled it. 'He's... What do you do again, darl?'

'Insurance,' said the large, hairy man. 'You've got a good pair of lungs on you, kid.'

He and my mother laughed a long time at that little joke. I

didn't want to be in the kitchen with them. I wrinkled my nose and took my cereal to eat in front of the television. He was not supposed to be in our house. Our house was too small for a man as big as him. It was only two bedrooms, and my mother slept in one and I slept in the other. I didn't know where he would sleep. I was very innocent. My mother tried, in her own way, to protect me from the world. Bernie never came back, and he's about the only name I remember in the parade that followed. I remember faces more. Faces, bodies, smells. There was a tall, thin man who sniffed constantly, and one who stank strongly of the insecticide he used all day in his work as an exterminator. There was the man who drank too much and fell asleep on the couch, and the one who kept telling me, 'Don't you touch my stuff,' like I had any interest in any of it. I probably do remember their names if I think about it enough, but why bother? None of them lasted very long and they were mostly harmless, just in my space and taking my mother's attention.

Mostly harmless, but not all of them. Not all of them.

My mother didn't want to have to keep working to take care of her only child. She wanted a husband, and she knew she needed to replace my father. I don't think about him much. There's no reason to, because I never really felt the loss of him. My mother was my whole world, and as long as she was there, I was fine. I worried when she got sick last year about how I would survive without her, but even though I grieve for her, even though I see her standing in doorways and sometimes wake to hear her calling me, she allowed me to stay trapped in this house, and I was never going to leave if I had her.

Today I wish she was still here and that I was still safe behind the front door, waiting for her to return with a stack of magazines and say, 'Here you go, love – for your collection.'

But she's not, and I was out, and I have seen things today and done things today and now... now I don't know what's going to happen.

'It's easy for a man, Ruth,' she told me when I got older, and asked about all the men she made friends with. 'A man can just leave, but a woman... a woman has to stay and take care of the children. Remember that if you ever fall in love.' It sounded like a curse, and I've made sure to never find myself in that position.

'Maybe if you found a better job and I found a job we wouldn't need anyone else,' I said when I was twelve.

'You're a laugh,' she told me. 'Just get yourself to school and let me worry about everything else.'

In between men, she and I had a lovely time. There was never enough money if she was out of work, which was often, because she grew easily bored and said things to managers that were inappropriate, like 'this store would be nothing without me' and 'I'm the best saleswoman here and don't you forget it' and 'I'm taking a week's holiday because I've had enough of this place'.

'I told him.' She would smirk as she and I sat eating dinner. When she was working, I came home to an empty house during the week, so I didn't mind when she was between jobs. She was the kind of mother who was happy to spend hours playing board games with me, happy to sit next to me and watch something on television, happy to hear about my day in great detail. But I always knew that another man would be along soon, another man who was possibly the solution to our problems – although such a man never appeared. Mostly, they ignored me or spoke to me with forced cordiality, as though I was a much younger child. *Hello, Ruth, and what are you studying at school? Do you like ice cream?* I was always polite, because I knew whoever was keeping her company would soon be gone. She wanted marriage and stability and you couldn't really pick that up in a bar on a week night.

By the time I was thirteen, I was able to babysit myself, so it made things easier for her and she was out a lot. I was happy enough to be alone. I had friends to call on the phone and homework to do. I was tall and skinny and wore my school skirt turned up at the waist to make it as short as possible, because all the girls did. But I had no interest in boys. They smelled funny and they were silly and I was never into silly. I liked books and had a small group of friends who were all reading the same fantasy series, which we discussed every lunchtime, sitting in a circle, dissecting characters' motivations.

It was the short turned-up skirt that changed my life, sent it spinning off in a different direction. Some nights I torture myself by trying to imagine the kind of life I could have had. I see a husband and children, a proper career and a house that is clean but free of my collections. Those are not good nights, but at thirteen I didn't know what could happen and I shouldn't have had to know. I was thirteen and a child, finally fitting in at school and not feeling lost any more.

One morning, my mother got up in time to see me before I left to catch the bus. She usually slept until the very last minute, then rushed around the house getting dressed for work. I liked to be up early, to have time for breakfast and a little reading before I left for school. But on this particular morning, she had a job interview and she was up early to prepare.

'That skirt is ridiculously short,' she told me as she sipped her cup of coffee and looked me up and down.

'All the girls have it this way,' I replied.

'Don't they tell you it's not allowed? The male teachers must find it a bit much if you all walk around like that.'

I sometimes amuse myself by wondering how any young girl would react to a statement like that today. I can imagine every Twitter troll in the world coming out to cancel my mother for suggesting that male teachers were looking at schoolgirls as anything except students to teach. But cancel her all you like. She was right.

I just laughed, 'There's one who really likes it. We call him Touchy Tony.'

My mother picked up her cigarette from the ashtray next to her and sucked deeply. In the morning light, she looked older than her thirty-five years. Wrinkles had started to appear and she had developed a double chin, but her smile still lit up her face.

She didn't smile when I mentioned Touchy Tony.

'Why do you call him that?' she asked warily.

I shrugged. 'He's just extra friendly. When he talks to you, he always stands really close and he puts his hand on your back or your shoulder and sometimes it slides down to your bum.' I laughed when I said this. At school we never thought to complain. He was a teacher and you didn't complain about your teachers to anyone except each other. It was self-defence, I think, for us to find him funny rather than anything else, for us to be able to laugh at him. We should have shouted and screamed and complained. We should have told anyone who would listen – but even telling my mother felt wrong, as though I had allowed her to see inside the private world of my school.

'That's disgusting,' she said, sitting up straight. 'Has anyone reported him? Does he teach you?'

'Yes, but don't worry, he's not interested in me. He likes girls with big boobs.' And in my mind that made it acceptable. He wasn't bothering me, so why bother him?

'Ruth,' she said sternly, 'that's unacceptable. What exactly is he doing?'

I was beginning to regret the decision to say anything to her. Tony Richardson was an open secret at school. A man who was very clever at getting away with behaviour that should never have been tolerated. If he'd ever attacked someone, really hurt a girl, he would have been fired and probably jailed. But he was never that stupid. Instead, his touches could be dismissed as accidents. Fingers brushed over a breast, a hand touching a leg for support as he stood up, a pat on the back that slid down. Nothing too major, we thought, nothing to make a big deal about. He told slightly dirty jokes that the boys really laughed at but that made the girls blush, and he was nice-looking, with blue eyes and curly hair. He was a young teacher, young enough to look like one of the older students on days when we were all allowed to come in casual clothes. And a lot of male behaviour at school when I was thirteen was unacceptable by today's standards. Boys used to come up behind us and pull our bra straps, letting them snap back, and that was considered an indication that you were liked by whoever had done it. Touchy Tony was just being extra, extra friendly.

Thinking about him now coils my stomach with unease and I regret eating lunch at all. While still listening to the policeman talking on the television, I get up and walk over to a pile of women's magazines, decorated with the smiling faces of A-, B- and C-list celebrities. I study the pile, taller than I am, and then I use my foot to push against it gently, gently until it topples. I enjoy the hissing rush of moving paper as everything tumbles to the ground, and then I sit on my haunches and smooth them out so no creases or dog ears appear on the pages. I begin restacking them. There are at least two decades' worth of magazines in the pile, and they are all as glossy and perfect as the day they were bought. Touchy Tony's face returns and I keep stacking so that I will not descend into panic. I keep an eye on the television, where pictures of the missing little girl appear in between questions being shouted out by reporters. I watch the mother in the background and I wait to have my suspicions confirmed as my hands slide over the slick magazine paper and the pile grows in front of me.

'I'm going to call the school and speak to him,' my mother told me all those years ago.

'Please don't,' I begged. 'This doesn't need to be a big deal. He doesn't bother me!'

'Fine,' she said, but I didn't believe her.

I was right not to. She called the school, she met with him

and he explained how it was all a misunderstanding. A short skirt, a blurted truth, a phone call and my life was hideously changed.

I realise now that the police officer has stopped answering questions. I missed the start of the press conference, so I assume that's when he gave out all the information needed.

People in the garden of the house, the large beautiful house that couldn't keep a little girl safe, begin to move away, but for some reason the camera keeps going, panning over the front garden, where a poor rose bush has been trampled to death.

I stop what I'm doing and watch carefully, and that's when I see it. The mother is standing off to the side, and it's almost accidental that she is even in the shot of the opulent home that belongs to her. As she stands there, he walks up to her and puts his arms around her, holding her tight for a moment before she moves away.

I nod my head. I was right then. I knew it was him. I imagine what life will be like for the missing little girl should she be found, should she grow up in a home with him as her father. I see him watching her as her body begins to change, watching and waiting. I see her distress, see her questioning herself, wondering if she's feeling uneasy all the time for a reason or if she's just imagining it. The anxiety of living with it all the time, of never being able to relax, will damage her beyond repair. I used to hope, to pray that he would just ignore me, that he would stop seeing me, but he never did. I wanted to be invisible, but if I couldn't be invisible, I needed to lock myself away, behind doors, behind my collections, protected by the things I piled up. I wouldn't want that for the little girl with black hair. I wouldn't want that for anyone.

My throat closes and I get up and quickly grab for my soda, forcing the pink liquid down. I put the can back on the coffee table and squeeze my hands into fists. I was right. I turn off the television. I don't need to see any more. I don't want to see any more. I was right.

I return to stacking the magazines, needing to create order and safety in my space. The piles keep him out of my head, out of my home. I need to stack quickly while I try to catch my breath, but eventually I am soothed by the repetition and the feel of slick paper in my hands.

What I've done is wrong, very wrong. I know that. But now that I'm sure he is her father, now that I've seen him, I think it makes it somehow strangely right.

CHAPTER TEN

LESLIE

4.15 p.m.

It's just after four, and Millie has been gone for... over three hours. After all the activity of the police arriving and the interviews and the press conference, everything is relatively quiet inside the house and there's a terrible feeling in the air of *now what?* Her little girl is not home. Twenty-one hours to go. The appearance on television has not allowed her to be miraculously located and brought home, and even though Leslie wants to go and scour the park and the neighbourhood herself, she has been told to stay put, and she cannot argue with the police, cannot disobey the police. They're not ready to issue the amber alert yet, but if Millie was just lost, she would have been found. How far can a three-year-old walk? How many people would see a small child walking alone and simply ignore her?

She would like to speak to Shelby in private, but Bianca is not letting anyone near her daughter. Leslie has a feeling that if she could just get a quiet moment with Shelby, the girl would tell her what really happened, because her explanation is obviously not completely true. Is it even slightly true? Bianca and

Shelby are sitting next to each other on the sofa, and every now and again, Leslie watches Bianca's eyes sweep around the living room, taking in the hand-woven Persian rugs that she has hung on the wall to lend the room colour and movement, and the heavy, lustrous blue curtains that frame the double-height windows. She can imagine Bianca's spitting anger were she to know that the soft grey suede sofa she is sitting on cost over ten thousand dollars. 'Just buy whatever you want,' Randall had told her. He was happy to give her absolutely everything, and she wonders occasionally why it's not enough for her, why she can't just be content being a stay-at-home mother and kept wife with a website that allows her to work a little. But the idea grates on her, and she can see herself disappearing into her role of mother and stepmother, of becoming someone who listens to other people explain their ideas and work days rather than being the one to speak.

'So, Shelby, just wanted to check something,' says Constable Dickerson, coming in from the kitchen, where he is making phone calls and directing searchers. Shelby sits up, her cheeks flushing. She is hiding something. Leslie can see it a mile away, and she wonders if the constable can as well.

Shelby nods her head.

'Millie's only a little thing, so we're just checking that she definitely opened the door herself. The front door is very big and heavy and the handle is above her head, so it would have been quite difficult for her.'

Leslie takes a deep breath and holds it, afraid to let the air out. Of course Millie wouldn't have been able to open the door herself. Why is this question only being asked now? Why hadn't she or Randall thought to ask it? What kind of mother is she? What kind of parents are they?

Shelby's face turns scarlet. 'Um, yes... I guess... I mean... a chair, she used a chair, her little chair.' She points at the small table and chairs, washed in a light purple, set up in a corner of the living room. 'Millie's space', the little girl calls it. When she's angry or sad about something, she tells Leslie that she has to wait to be invited into her space. 'I don't want to talk,' she will say, waving her hand, and Leslie knows to wait until some drawing or colouring has worked its magic of making her daughter feel better.

Leslie can imagine Millie dragging one of the little wooden chairs to the front door, because she often uses them to raise herself up to where she needs to be. But the door is very heavy and she would have had to keep pulling on it, moving the chair back until she had opened it enough to slip out. Surely by then Shelby would have been back from the bathroom? And there is a bathroom on this level. There are two, in fact. Why did Shelby need to go upstairs? She could have used the bathroom tucked away behind the kitchen and the laundry. She could have used the one attached to Randall's study. Why did she go upstairs? Leslie wills the constable to ask these questions. *Ask her*, she wants to scream, *ask her why she's lying. Ask her where my child is.*

Constable Dickerson nods his head but doesn't say anything.

'I mean, she left the chair there and I put it back. I just forgot to tell you.'

'Okay, that would have been good to know. So just checking now – you didn't look for her immediately?'

'I don't... I can't remember,' says Shelby, and tears bubble up in her eyes. She turns her head to her mother and buries her face in her shoulder, shutting out the constable and – Leslie is sure – shutting out the truth.

Leslie closes her hands, pushes her nails into her palms. She is struggling to control herself, to control her need to yell at Shelby to tell them what happened, what really happened. Could Shelby have lashed out at her little sister for some reason? Lashed out and hurt her and then... She feels her hand stray up to her hair and quickly folds her arms. Shelby is a child, just a child, and she wouldn't have hurt her sister, but Leslie is running out of other things to imagine.

'Why did you go upstairs to use the bathroom, Shelby?' she asks, the words leaping from her mouth. She has tried to moderate her tone to indicate simple curiosity, but her voice is strained, her anger obvious.

Shelby stops crying abruptly and looks at her. 'What?' she asks, her tears disappearing, her jaw tense.

'Yes, right,' says the constable without looking at Leslie. 'We did want to check on that…' He stops speaking and glances back at Leslie, and she understands that she has done something wrong, interrupted and asked a question the constable has been saving for a better time or something, but she doesn't care. All these questions should have been asked immediately, should have been asked by *her* the moment she came home and finished searching the house. Maybe then Millie would be home and safe, maybe Shelby would have confessed to whatever it is she has done, maybe all of this would be over. She's not going to stop talking because the constable has some agenda he won't share with them. This is her daughter – her daughter – and she will scream questions until she's blue in the face if she has to.

'What a ridiculous, stupid question to ask my child,' Bianca hisses, her cheeks colouring, her eyes narrowing. 'You have no right to be angry at her, to accuse her of anything. *You* left *your* child and went swanning off to the shops. I never did that. I never left my child alone with anyone except her father, and after the divorce she was with me twenty-four-seven, and you think that a trip to the shops justifies putting a twelve-year-old girl in charge of a recalcitrant toddler? How dare you?' Her anger strangles the words as the colour on her face spreads down her neck. She holds Shelby closer to her, protecting her from the big, bad stepmother.

Pre-schooler, thinks Leslie, making sure to keep her mouth closed. Not a toddler, not recalcitrant, not naughty. Just a lovely ray of sunshine, a beautiful blessing, my baby girl. She wraps her arms tighter around her body, sent back into silence by Bianca's fury, hating herself for allowing the woman to be in her home, in Millie's home. Her face burns with humiliation. She has allowed Bianca to speak to her as though she is the child, and she has allowed it to happen in her own home, in the home she created as a sanctuary for her family. She wants to howl and run at her. She hangs her head instead, studies her shoes, her flat black shoes. She changed into a different outfit before the police arrived, ran upstairs quickly and put on jeans and a warm jumper, thinking she would be going out searching. The smart black pants and tight red top she had been wearing lie crumpled on the bathroom floor, filling the air with the jasmine-scented perfume she applied liberally this morning as she hummed to herself. She had been, she feels, an entirely different person then, a person she will never be again. She needs to speak to Randall about that, about what she did, needs to tell him before somehow someone else does. But she cannot see how to get him alone without everyone questioning her need for secrets.

'Can I get you something?' Constable Willow asks whenever she moves.

'Is there anything you need?' Constable Dickerson said gently when she started to follow Randall outside only ten minutes ago. They seem to be actively trying to keep her and Randall from being alone with each other.

'Let's just leave this now,' says Constable Dickerson gently, motioning up and down with his hands as though tamping down the tension in the room.

Leslie feels herself to be physically smaller; her body has shrunk with each sentence uttered by Bianca, with each statement from the detective, with each hour that has passed, and she is glad that Randall is not here but outside talking to neighbours and those involved in the search.

The constable stands up and walks away. Leslie wants to follow him and ask him what he's thinking, but he is quickly surrounded by other constables who have arrived to help.

She moves to the window of the living room, away from Bianca's poisonous stare. 'Get out of my house,' she mutters under her breath, over and over. *Get out of my house, get out of my house, get out of my house.*

From the window, she can see her crowded front yard. She watches the reporters standing in groups on the bright green lawn, interviewing searchers and the police, keeping the story going when nothing is happening. Two men and a woman stand together, peering down at their phones, and then there is suddenly a burst of laughter that makes Leslie feel sick. But if they have children, they know where they are, so why shouldn't they laugh at today's favourite meme or whatever it is they are looking at?

The police are constantly asking the people who are helping with the search to remain outside. Constable Willow keeps saying, 'If you could please just congregate on the front lawn' every time he passes someone who has just walked in, making themselves part of the drama. Some she knows, some she doesn't, but those she does know all offer skin-crawling hugs. They mean to be kind but she can't take it.

'I'm so sorry, Leslie,' says a woman who has somehow found her way into the house, despite the ever-vigilant constables.

Leslie grits her teeth and turns from the window to see someone from Millie's ballet class. Is there anyone who has not heard her daughter is missing? How did the news spread so fast, and why is this woman here?

'Thank you,' she says.

The woman smiles. 'What a lovely house you have.'

Leslie has no idea how to reply, so she turns back to the window, hoping that her rudeness will be forgiven.

Do these people just want to gawk and gossip? Do they really want to help or are they here to witness her failure? Even Trevor, Bianca's new husband, has arrived. 'You don't need to be here,' Leslie heard Bianca telling him.

'It's a missing kid, B, more people looking is a good thing,' he replied.

'What a lot of trouble this child has caused,' Bianca said, sniffing as though she could smell something off in the house, knowing that Leslie could hear her. Trevor threw her an apologetic look, but she turned away.

Leslie has always believed in giving people the benefit of the doubt. When she hears gossip about someone at school, or an old friend, she tries to see it from their perspective. Those who cheat and lie and hurt others usually have their reasons. Their own hurt, their own fear, or something damaging in their past. This is always the first thing she thinks about. And she has tried to do this with Bianca, knowing that the woman has some right to her anger at her ex-husband. She has tried to see things from Bianca's perspective, to view her with some empathy, but the woman makes it very, very hard. And now, at a time when all she has to do is sit quietly and encourage her daughter to tell the truth, she seems to be intent on hampering, minimising and diminishing the investigation and the seriousness of Millie being missing. Her concern is only for herself – even her tight hold on Shelby appears more for her own sake than for Shelby's comfort.

Leslie leans her head briefly against the glass of the window before someone looks at her from the garden and she straightens up. There are parents from Millie's pre-school class here as well. One woman even brought her child, which strikes Leslie as bizarre.

She can't stand here any longer, and she turns and goes to

find the constable. He is in the kitchen, on the phone, nodding his head as though the person he is speaking to can see him. She waits patiently until he finishes his call.

'I want to go and look for her,' she says. 'I know there are a lot of people out there, but I want to go and look. Maybe she's scared and hiding and if I call her she will come to me.' She makes sure to stand up straight, to keep her shoulders back and her voice strong. She is tired of being told what to do.

'Right, I understand that, but I need you to stay here in case someone calls you.'

'Who would call?' she asks, bewildered. 'If Millie is found by someone and she tells them my mobile number – because she knows it – I'll have my phone with me, so why can't I go and look for her?' She hears Millie's voice, high in a sing-song repetition of her phone number, all the way to pre-school and back, again and again, until Leslie was certain the number was imprinted on her mind. She wills the phone in her hand to ring, but it remains silent. 'She knows my number,' she repeats.

'Yes, and that's good,' says the constable, 'but the thing is... Well, we've been discussing your husband's business, and it's... it's a big business and there may be some people who...'

'Who would what?' she asks, frustrated by what the constable is not saying.

'If she has been taken or picked up by someone, they may call and it's possible that... that they may ask for money.'

'What? Like a ransom?' She feels a bubble of laughter inside her at the absurdity of such a thing.

'Your wealth, your husband's business... all of that makes you a possible target. It may not be the case at all, not at all, but... we have to consider it.'

His serious tone instantly dissolves the bubble of laughter inside her, turning it to acid in her stomach. She has never considered that this could be a possibility. This is Australia. Things like that don't happen here. Do they?

How can her husband be a target because of his wealth? He's never hurt anyone. He's generous with charitable donations and it's not as if they live a big life. Their house is large and new but they don't go out much and they are certainly not seen at expensive restaurants or parties where the rich and famous go. How can they be a target? How can *Millie* be a target? Leslie presses her hand to her lips. She's not going to throw up.

'If that's the case,' she says slowly, taking a deep breath, 'if you really think that could have happened, then you need to issue the amber alert.'

'Right, yes... we've just done that, Leslie. We've just done it.' His gaze is kind, filled with sympathy, and Leslie would like to fall into his arms and howl on his shoulder. She has no father or mother to comfort her, and Randall is struggling as well. She is completely, terribly alone, and the thought of someone stealing her child for money is horrifying and disgusting in equal measure.

'Oh... oh God,' she says, and she turns and flees the kitchen.

The amber alert means this is now something else, something more sinister, more terrible. It can't be possible and yet it is. She returns to the living room and sees Bianca on the sofa with Shelby, and she wants to run, to leave this house and just run, but she can't go anywhere. She goes back to the window. Does Randall know what the police are thinking? Have they told him?

'Thanks for... thanks for helping,' she hears him say to someone, through the slightly open window. His voice breaks a little, and as she watches, Leslie can read utter defeat and despair on his face. If Millie is not found, if their precious child does not come home, she knows it will be the end for them.

Millie's birth was a miracle, as is the birth of every child. Leslie was already thirty-five when they began trying, not so old but old enough to know it might be difficult. It had been a condition of their marriage that she have a child and they had begun trying even before she donned her simple white dress and they exchanged vows. She had made Randall agree before saying yes to his rather underwhelming proposal. *So, what do you think of maybe getting married?* They had been waiting for a tow truck at the time. Randall's expensive new Jaguar had broken down and the roadside assistance man had been unable to get it back on the road. They had been heading out to grab a pizza, after a Saturday of lounging around Leslie's apartment, doing nothing much. Leslie was dressed in sweat pants, her face make-up-free, her hair tied back.

'What?' she had asked, sure she had misheard. And instead of repeating himself, he'd just shrugged, making her laugh.

'I want to have a child,' she'd replied as the tow truck drove towards them.

'Okay,' he'd said simply, flagging the man down.

The night after Millie was born, he'd been sitting next to her hospital bed, keeping her company at three in the morning as she struggled to get her fussy baby to latch on. 'Thank you for giving me another child, for giving me another daughter,' he had said.

If Millie does not come home, she and Randall will never recover from this, never be able to go on, never be able to function again. She knows that with absolute certainty.

CHAPTER ELEVEN

SHELBY

'Can you please just eat something?' says her mother, and Shelby is so tired of hearing those words that she picks up the sandwich her mother has made and placed in front of her. It felt weird watching her open and close cupboards and the fridge, finding everything she needed, and even as she made the sandwich Shelby heard her mutter, 'A dream kitchen for a dream house,' and then saw her shake her head.

Her mother made her move from the sofa to the kitchen so that they could be away from Leslie, who is staring out of the living room window as if Millie is going to just walk up the street. Her mother didn't actually say that. She said, 'I've had enough of being stared at – how about you?' and then she stood up. Shelby could have stayed in the living room, but she feels better if she's next to her mother, as though she won't accidentally let something slip. Her mother keeps telling her she doesn't have to talk to anyone, she doesn't have to say anything, she doesn't have to explain. And Shelby is listening to her, partly because she is so scared, partly because every time she hears the words, she warns herself to keep quiet. She's managed to evade and kind of lie every time the constable has spoken to her.

Millie never used a chair. Shelby actually never went upstairs to the bathroom. She wasn't alone, although no one has asked her if she was, so that's a lie by omission. She just hasn't told anyone. Does that make it a worse lie or a better lie? She can never remember.

She takes a bite of the sandwich. It's cheese and salad, so she takes another bite. At least it's not meat. She and Kiera have decided that they are going to become vegetarians after they saw the most awful thing on YouTube about how cows are treated. It made her sick to her stomach and she felt so sorry for the poor animals that she vowed to never eat meat again. So far, she hasn't told her mother or father about this. She just pushes the meat on her plate to one side and eats everything else. She will tell them when she feels like it. But lately she doesn't feel like talking to either of them. Lately she's often lost in thought, trying to figure out a way to make things better, but it's not working. Leslie has started cooking more vegetarian dishes without saying anything except that she 'thought it might be a nice change'. She knows, Shelby is sure she knows, but she won't say anything.

Shelby swallows a mouthful of guilt with her sandwich, hating that this has happened, knowing that if she says anything, if she tells the truth, then a lot more people are going to get hurt. She promised to keep quiet. She promised not to tell, and she hasn't. But it's so hard to watch everyone in this house and know that you're the one responsible for all this sadness. She feels the bite of sandwich threaten to come up and she gulps down some water. All this was supposed to be over by now. Why is it going on so long? They should have found her. It wasn't like she was going to go anywhere.

'How long do we have to stay here?' Bianca asks Trevor, who is standing next to her in the kitchen. He has just come back from looking around the neighbourhood. Shelby turns away from them, the sandwich in her hand even though she knows she's not going to eat another bite. This is just an irritating situation to her mother, something that's getting in the way of her Saturday afternoon with Trevor.

What happened keeps going through her head, a series of images getting darker and darker until there is only the black space of what is going to happen now. She cannot find the picture for that one because she has no idea. After Kiera called, it had only taken her ten minutes to get to the house. Shelby was in awe. Her own parents wouldn't let her catch a bus by herself. 'There was one just waiting right outside my front gate, so lucky,' Kiera had said. 'Wow, I forget how big this house is. Your dad is so, so rich. OMG, you won't believe it, but some guy on the bus tried to talk to me and I just... closed my eyes and pretended to be asleep,' she laughed. Kiera always talks quickly, always says a lot, believing that everything she has to say is interesting.

Millie had been standing quietly by Shelby's side, listening and watching, ever since Shelby opened the front door to reveal Kiera standing there, casually dressed in jeans and a multi-coloured long-sleeved top, with two earrings in each ear, looking older than she was.

'Hi, Kiera, me and Shelby is going to draw pictures together after my nails dry,' she said when Kiera stopped speaking. She loved it when Shelby had friends over, loved playing with the big girls. And most of Shelby's friends tolerated her, but not Kiera.

'Why don't you go and watch a movie? Shelby and I need to talk.' She didn't even look at Millie when she said it. 'Have you got anything to drink?' she asked Shelby, and started heading for the kitchen, as though the house belonged to her.

'I don't want to,' Millie said. 'Shelby is my babysitter today and we're going to draw.'

Kiera stopped walking and turned around to look at her. 'Yeah, well she's my best friend and she wants to do something else. She doesn't want to be your babysitter.' And then she stuck her tongue out at Millie, who gasped. Leslie lectured Millie a lot on being polite, on saying please and thank you and answering when someone spoke to you. She'd been told that sticking out her tongue at someone was rude, and she was such an obedient child, she had never done it to anyone.

Shelby had laughed without meaning to, torn between loving the idea that Kiera had called her her best friend and wanting to tell her to stop arguing with a three-year-old.

'She's my friend too,' said Millie, and her bottom lip drooped. Shelby could see she was getting ready to cry.

'Let's just draw,' she said to Kiera. 'We can talk while we draw.' She moved over to Millie's little purple-painted table with the matching chairs and sat down, her knees up near her chest because the chair was so small.

'No, I didn't come here for that,' Kiera said, her hands on her hips.

'Come on, K, just for a few minutes.'

'No, I got myself all the way here and your step-monster will be home soon. I need to talk to you in private. Jason messaged me on Instagram yesterday and I wanted to show you.'

Shelby bit down on her lip. Jason was really cute and he was the first boy in their year who seemed to be interested in talking to girls. The other boys were more into playing soccer at lunch, but Jason seemed older and Shelby had kind of a crush on him. If he liked Kiera, that was fine, but she really wanted to know what they talked about, since she was sure that when it came to talking to a boy – talking to a boy she really liked – she would totally suck at it. It was easy enough to talk to boys who were just boys and not boys she liked.

'I want to draw,' repeated Millie, used to having Shelby do what she wanted when they were together. 'You sit down now and draw, Kiera. Me and Shelby are going to draw rainbows.'

'I don't want to draw with you,' said Kiera, looking at her phone.

'It will only be for a few minutes,' pleaded Shelby, not wanting to upset her little sister.

'I don't want to.' Kiera looked up and actually stamped her foot. 'I came to talk to you and I don't need a baby listening to what we're saying,' she yelled, her frustration obvious. Shelby felt bad for letting her come when she knew she would have to take care of Millie, and she was momentarily irritated with her little sister and her stepmother for making her babysit. She really wanted to see what Jason had said.

'You mustn't shout,' said Millie, a tear on her cheek.

Shelby's irritation dissolved immediately. She hated it when Millie cried. She never shouted or screamed, just cried quietly, which was sad to watch. 'Please don't cry, Millie Billy, we can draw,' she said desperately, regretting allowing Kiera to come over.

'No, Shelby, don't give in to her. She's just being a brat. Go and watch a movie, you little pain in the butt.'

'I'm going to tell my mum on you,' cried Millie.

'Your mum won't care,' said Kiera, and she stuck her tongue out at her again while pulling an ugly face.

'Okay,' said Shelby, 'I think that's enough. We can all go and watch a movie.'

'I don't want to. I want to draw, and if you don't draw with me, I'll... I'll run away.'

Shelby laughed, because Millie was always threatening to run away when she didn't like the way things were going. Leslie always said, 'Well, I'll pack you some food to take with you, and I'll come too, because you can't run away without your mum.' And that always made Millie laugh.

But this time, Kiera strode over to the front door and opened it and said, 'Well go on then, you little brat. Run.' And then there had been a moment, just a moment, when everything could have been different, where if Shelby had grabbed her little sister, today would still be an ordinary day, where if she'd moved fast enough, Millie would still be here.

She has never hated Millie. Even when she has been annoyed by her, she has loved her. No one in the world makes her feel more seen than Millie, even Kiera. When she comes over to stay, she'll walk through the front door and Millie will be bouncing with excitement. 'Shelby, Shelby, Shelby, you're here, you're here. I've got so many secrets to tell you.' Millie's secrets usually involve sneaking an extra lolly when Leslie has told her she can only have one, and secretly looking at her books past her bedtime, but she loves sharing everything with Shelby. One weekend when Shelby was staying over, Millie had a friend to play. They had walked past Shelby's bedroom on their way to Millie's room and Shelby had heard her say, 'That's my big sister's room and she is the smartest, bestest person I know.' She had felt a warm glow of love for her sister. Millie loved her completely and unconditionally, and no one else in the world did that.

The only good thing about her parents getting divorced has been the arrival of Millie, not that she would tell anyone that.

When Millie was born, her dad took her to visit Leslie and the baby in the hospital and she had stood looking down at her with a teddy clutched in her hand and wondered why everyone thought babies were so special.

'Do you want to hold her?' her dad asked, and she had shrugged her shoulders because she didn't really care. But then he had picked up the small wrapped bundle and placed her in Shelby's arms, and she had felt the light weight of her and smelled the biscuit smell of her, and then Millie had opened her eyes and fixed them on Shelby's face. Something like a smile, which everyone knew was wind, had appeared on the baby's face and Shelby had felt her heart lurch with love.

She would have done anything to protect her little sister,

even though she grumbled about having to take care of her. Anything. But she'd failed to do that and she has a feeling that tomorrow, when the sun comes up, her whole life will be shattered and her family gone. She should never have had Kiera over, should never have let her talk to Millie like that.

She should have been braver and stronger and protected her little sister, instead of it being the other way around.

CHAPTER TWELVE

RUTH

It was a chance sighting. It's always a chance sighting, isn't it? Just a quick glance in a coffee shop and the shock of recognition. Before I recognised him, I was feeling very proud of myself. *Well done, Ruth*, I was repeating to myself, because I always congratulate myself for getting out of the house and going into a shop. It helps with the mounting anxiety, as I stand and wait to be served and wait to pay and wait to get myself back out into the street and home again. *Well done, Ruth*. I always go to the same coffee shop and order the same thing: a large latte made with almond milk with a dash of caramel flavouring – delicious and sweet, comfort in every mouthful, and easy to drink cold when I get home and need to settle myself again.

I wish I could explain to people how difficult it is to go out, to leave my safe space with my neat piles, but even if I could, there is no one to listen any more. Before I leave, I allow myself fifteen minutes of pile-stacking so that I am calm and composed, and then I walk to the coffee shop. I don't make eye contact. I don't speak to anyone except to order and say thank you. And I am careful to be forever watchful.

When I return from being out, I don't drink my coffee until I have knocked over and restacked at least three piles. I like the number three, double three, triple three. Only then, when my heart rate is slow and steady and my breathing even, do I drink. Sometimes when it's very bad, I remind myself that I wasn't always like this. Even after it started happening, I was still able to leave the house. But then it took over and I was never safe, not in my bedroom, not in the bathroom. I never allowed myself to sleep, only dropping into an exhausted black hole when I had no choice. I would go days without a shower because I felt exposed when I took my clothes off, felt thousands of eyes watching me, saw staring spectres everywhere. I moved around my own home like an intruder, hoping not to be spotted, even when I was alone. And I started making piles. In the end, they were what made me feel better; they kept me safe. I surrounded myself with large piles of books, stacks of T-shirts, collections of rocks from the garden. It was hard to get into my bedroom at night, and if I wanted to go to the bathroom, I had to switch on the light so that I didn't trip over something.

'This is ridiculous,' my mother said. 'You need to clean it all up.' But I refused. I couldn't explain, couldn't reveal what I was holding inside me. Some of it was to protect her. My mother's life was hard, made harder by having me and being the one who stayed. I wanted her to be happy. I didn't want to burden her with my secrets, my terrible, ugly secrets.

I have a feeling that at some point she gave up and hoped that I would somehow fix myself. I have been getting better, little by little, especially since she is no longer here to protect me from the outside world, or expose me to those she brought into my world.

But then I saw him again.

Seeing him in the coffee shop was a coincidence. Life is filled with coincidences, most of them nasty. It's why I don't leave the house if I can help it, although lately... well, I've been on a bit of a mission. Lately I have been the one watching him. That feels... better somehow. He doesn't know. When I watch him, follow him, I always have a large bag with me, heavy and filled with my collection of black tourmaline stones. They are for healing and protection, and if I sense the anxiety rising, I stuff my hand in the bag and feel their cool smoothness. It's a portable pile. Once, when I was far from home in my little yellow car, I felt my breathing start to go awry, and I pulled over and upended my bag onto the passenger seat and made heap after heap of the stones until I was better.

There were two ways I could have gone after I saw him. I could have retreated into my home and never left again. You can do that nowadays. Everything arrives at your doorstep through the internet, except the doctor and the dentist – and even as I had the thought, my tongue touched my painful tooth, sending a little shock through my body. But in the same way I need to make my piles, I knew I needed to prevent myself from retreating. His decades-long hold over my life could not go on. My mother's lament – *what is wrong with you, what is wrong with you, what is wrong with you?* – filled my dreams.

And so instead of retreat, I chose the other option. The other option was attack. And an attack needs planning.

I left the house, I followed him, observed him, studied him. He used to be the cat, tormenting little mouse me. I had to be watchful and wary whenever I left my safe space, in case he was waiting to pounce. But now this little mouse has not returned to her safe house, although perhaps I should have. Perhaps then I wouldn't be avoiding the news right now for fear of seeing his wife's distress, knowing what I know. She has no idea how much worse things could get.

I never thought I would see him again, and when I did, what bothered me most was that I was instantly a child again, vulnerable, unprotected, unsafe.

Touchy Tony. Still handsome, still tall, but now a little more distinguished-looking because of the grey threads in his curly hair. Still Touchy Tony but at the same time not him at all.

He'd never noticed me before my mother went to the school to confront him, puffed up with determination, her face made up in bright colours, a tight top revealing cleavage. The night after that, she sat me down at the dinner table and said, 'Listen, Ruth. You and your friends have to stop talking about this man like this. He is doing nothing wrong and you're going to ruin his reputation. You may even end up getting him fired, and then he would have no job and he wouldn't be able to support himself. He explained to me that it's all nonsense and he's always targeted because you young girls develop a crush and then get nasty.'

I almost had to admire the way he had twisted her thinking. She went there enraged and indignant and returned home one of his greatest defenders. He was terribly charming to the mothers of all the girls, made them smile on parent–teacher nights, made them nod along with him as he discussed his concern for their little girls, made them believe every word out of his mouth. My mother was in sales and you would think she would have recognised a master manipulator, being something of a manipulator herself when it came to pushing people into a purchase. But she'd never met a salesman like Touchy Tony. He was selling himself and his honesty and his desire to help, and he was very, very good at it.

A thirteen-year-old today would have said, 'What rubbish.' She would have texted her friends and they would have annihilated him over Snapchat and Twitter and Instagram. They would have banded together and driven him out, but then, twenty-five years ago, we were less forceful, less certain of our own opinions, less comfortable confronting an older man, especially one that a lot of us did actually have a crush on.

The next day, after she'd gone to see him, he asked me to

stay in at lunch and said, 'I've had a chat with your mother and cleared everything up. I hope we can be friends.'

And I stuttered and mumbled and nodded my head. He looked down at me, kindness in his blue eyes that seemed tinged with just a little sympathy for my silly accusations. I felt forgiven and glad of his forgiveness. I didn't want to be responsible for him losing his job.

'I'm sorry,' I managed to mutter. I can't believe it of myself now when I think back on it, but that's what happened. I apologised. To him. I apologised to him.

Later, after school, he pulled up next to me in his car while I was walking home from the bus stop and said, 'I didn't know you and your mother lived around here. Can I give you a lift?'

The words 'no thanks' wanted to burst out of my mouth. My legs twitched, because all I wanted to do was run and all I could feel was my racing heart, but I said, 'Yes, thanks' and got into his silver car. He still drives a silver car, different make but the same colour. And his hand went to my knee, gave it a little pat, slid up my thigh a bit until I crossed my legs. Then he returned it to the steering wheel and laughed to himself. He knew what he was doing.

In the coffee shop, I didn't notice him at first, but then the barista called a name and I looked up from my phone, where I was watching a video of a dog going from abandoned stray to healthy, happy family pet, because I need to do that when I'm waiting to order so the anxiety doesn't bubble out of my mouth and lead me to screaming at everyone to get away from me. I looked up because... because you always do, just to see how many people are before you, and he said, 'Yes, here,' and just like that, there he was, standing practically next to me. It wasn't his name the barista called, but he took the coffee. I stood staring with my mouth open as the barista said, 'What can I get you?' more than once. And because the barista asked me a few times, he looked up from putting his card back into his wallet and looked right at me. And then he nodded and smiled and went on his way. I stepped back and let the person behind me place their order as I struggled to get control of my breathing, pinpricks dancing up and down my arms. He hadn't recognised me. He looked straight at me and didn't even recognise me. I was nothing to him. He left me a husk of a person and he didn't even have the decency to remember me.

I left without my coffee, fury coursing in my veins, making me hot in the cold air. I think I walked up and down the same stretch of pavement outside my house for an hour, not caring who saw, my arms swinging as the sky clouded over with swollen grey clouds, threatening a storm that never came. I'm sure that I looked slightly mad, muttering to myself about how vile he was, how he would pay. My body shuddered as I remembered the little touches, the small invasions that had broken me down.

A thousand tiny assaults made me who I am today. And because they were so very small, I can never point to one traumatic incident and say, 'That's what happened to me.' Touches and taps and pushes and leers and words that shouldn't be said. Nothing big, nothing major, but taken together, they destroyed who I was.

At some point I started writing them down, but I stopped when I filled three journals. *Today he brushed up against me. Today he told me a dirty joke. Today he rested his hand on my breast for a few seconds.*

I thought it was over when he left my life, but it is never going to be over. And seeing him again – the terrible coincidence of seeing him again – nearly killed me.

When I finally went inside my home that day, I had to knock over many, many piles before a sense of calm returned. It took thirty-three piles, large and small, heavy and light, soft and hard, before I could inhale and exhale normally. I was knocking over and restacking things late into the night. But finally, when I was done, I made a decision. I would follow him and find him and expose him to the world. I was pretty sure he would still be doing the same thing. A cat will always chase a mouse, the strong will always prey on the weak, and Touchy Tony would still be finding young girls to lean against, his hot breath in their ears. I would follow him and expose him to the world, finally expose him, and I would not be silenced, because I was not thirteen or fourteen or fifteen now. Why not? I had nothing else to do. He had made sure that I had nothing else to do.

And now the time has come, because although I don't like what has happened to his daughter, it allows me to shine a glaring bright light on him and what he's done. He should never have been allowed to have a child, to raise a little girl, especially one as pretty as the girl they are all searching for.

On the television, he hugged his wife, hard and tight, supporting her in their grief. I look up the child's mother's name on my phone. She's a graphic designer with her own website, and her mobile number is right there, neat black numbers set out for anyone at all to call. Perhaps she has a separate work phone, but I doubt it. People live on their phones and only need a second one for nefarious activities like being a drug dealer. I saw that on television.

I slowly type my message out, needing to let her know. If she knows, she can leave him, expose him, report him to the police so he is locked up. And then when the little girl is found, she will be safe from him. I don't say much. She will reply and then I will explain. I immediately start arranging the words in my head, the way I will explain things to her. I wait for a moment, a sense of the world shifting inside me. Once it's sent, it cannot be unsent. She will know who he is, she will know what he's done and she will know what he's doing now.

Touchy Tony – once a teacher, now a millionaire.

Once a man with no children of his own, now a father of a missing child.

Once a paedophile, always a paedophile.

The world needs to know.

I take a breath and hit send, and off it goes.

CHAPTER THIRTEEN

LESLIE

5.00 p.m.

There is, she reflects, nothing worse than waiting. Time refuses to stop as it moves past 5 p.m. and the sun drops lower in the sky. She has tried hiding in the study and she has tried occupying herself with tidying up after those who have been in her kitchen, touching things and moving things and changing things. Bianca is walking in and out, confident ownership in the way she is making cups of tea for the constables and food for Shelby. She has not offered Leslie anything.

'Get out,' she wants to scream at everyone, 'just get out.' Now she is sitting on the sofa, staring down at the carpet, wishing she could lie down on the soft blue pile and howl.

'Um, excuse me, Leslie,' says Constable Dickerson, pulling her from her thoughts.

She jerks up, the adrenaline of expectation rushing through her veins. 'Have they found her?' she asks.

'They haven't, but we are doing everything in our power to bring her home to you. Right now, I wanted to speak to you about your trip to the shops. Just a few quick questions if you don't mind.'

Leslie bites down on her lip. What have they found out? 'Yes,' she says cautiously.

'Right, well CCTV has you entering the shopping centre car park at one p.m., not twelve as you stated. Can you tell us where you were for the hour before that?' He asks the question politely, sure that there will be an explanation, but Constable Willow is standing beside him, his pen and little notebook in his hand, ready to record her answer.

Her face heats with a flush. 'I...'

'What's this about?' asks Randall, coming into the living room from outside. She had wanted to go out and stand in the cold with him, but she got the sense that the police preferred to keep them separate, preferred them not speaking to each other. The more they are treated like suspects, the more she feels a creeping sense of guilt. If she had gone straight to the shops and returned home, Millie would be here now – it's as simple as that.

'I'm just asking your wife about her timing today. CCTV has her entering the shopping centre an hour later than she said, so we wanted to clear that up.' The constable gives Randall a tight smile.

'Les?' says Randall, looking at her, his confusion obvious, and she's grateful that no one is sitting close to her. A build-up of sweat in her armpits makes her shift uncomfortably on the sofa.

'I met someone,' she whispers.

'Right, sorry, did you say you met someone? Just making sure I heard you correctly.' The constable raises his voice a little, obviously hoping to get her to raise hers.

'Yes,' says Leslie, looking up and meeting his gaze. *A secret kept is a secret you live to regret.* That's what this bitter taste in her mouth is – regret.

'Perhaps you could explain,' says Constable Willow. His voice is high, and when she looks over at him, she can see that she has assumed he's older than he is. His skin is lightly pink and he probably only needs to shave every other day. She has wondered at his silence in most interactions, except for quiet offers of tea, but now she understands: he is brand new to this. Brand new and inexperienced. Perhaps this is his first missing child case. Perhaps when he and Constable Dickerson go off shift, they will discuss what Constable Willow learned on the very worst day of Leslie's life. Perhaps his youth makes no difference because nothing can change the fact that Leslie should have been here at home instead of anywhere else.

She sits up straight. 'I met a man I used to work with named Graham; he used to be my boss.' There is no point in lying – they'll find out anyway.

'Right, and will he confirm that?' the constable asks.

She nods her head.

'Used to be your boyfriend as well, didn't he?' says Randall, crossing his arms. 'Of all the days to do that, Les...' He stops speaking and turns away from her, and then leaves the room.

Randall is not one for confrontation. He's told her that any argument he had with his first wife always ended with him apologising, and now he refuses to argue with Leslie. He walks away or agrees or just says sorry before she can even begin. Bianca had called him 'spineless'. A nasty term. Leslie prefers to think of him as a pacifist. He'll do anything to keep the peace. But sometimes she doesn't want to keep the peace; sometimes she would like a discussion, even an argument, because she finds that instead of defending her position, she simply swallows her feelings, and that's not good. It's something they need to work on as a couple. They need to learn how to argue with each other and stay married – but now is not the right time for any discussion at all. She's hurt him and she never meant to.

'It's not what you think,' she calls to his retreating form, but he keeps going. Shame and guilt rise up inside her. She has hurt him by not telling him. And now their daughter is missing. He stops just before he walks out of the front door and shakes his head at her. She can feel a shift in him, the blame for their missing child now heavier on her.

'Can I get his number, if you don't mind?' says Constable Willow, his pen ready to go.

Leslie looks up the number on her phone and hands it to the constable. There is nothing on her phone that he can't see. The constable taps the number into his own phone, carrying hers with him as he steps away to speak to Graham. She should have just said something at the beginning, but it had nothing to do with what happened to Millie, except for the very important fact that if she'd just been gone an hour, her little girl would still be here. But people run late, and it could have just been a long line at the store. It could have been. Her neck aches with the weight of all this guilt, and she would like to ask Constable Dickerson or Randall or Bianca if they have ever run late in their lives. The lines at the grocery store could have been longer than usual. A spark of indignation burns inside her. She was running late but her child was with someone she thought she could trust to take care of her. Why is this only and entirely her fault?

The whole encounter with Graham was thoroughly awkward anyway. They had met at a coffee shop Millie loved because it was decorated with pictures of all different kinds of cats. Walking in had been uncomfortable, but she had immediately spotted him, his large frame hunched in a corner, his gaze concentrated on his phone. The first word that always came to mind when she thought of Graham was 'shaggy'. His hair was too long, his shirt never tucked in, his pants always had a stain on them from lunch, but his smile made her feel completely seen, and when she had worked for him at the advertising agency, she had felt that every word out of her mouth was gold.

He told her in front of people and he told her in bed that she was brilliant and wonderful. When she first met Randall, she and Graham had only just broken up. It hadn't felt like it was going anywhere to her, and she was surprised that he felt differently, but she had suggested a break anyway. Her relationship with Randall had devastated him and she had found herself consoling him as he tried not to cry in her office when she told him she was seeing someone. 'But I love you,' he had said, bewildered that this was not enough. She had replied, 'But you never said, not really, and I want children and a marriage and a life.' Things that she only found she desperately wanted after meeting Randall.

'I would have given you all that. I mean, I would have had the discussion at least. You never even really asked me, and I would have had the conversation. And even if I don't want children, I love you – isn't that enough?'

At the time, Leslie had felt mostly irritated, but as years have gone by, the relationship has acquired a rosy glow in her memory.

He looked the same as he always had. She shouldn't have been speaking to him, but he had texted to ask how her website was doing and she had admitted that it was slow going; the business that came her way was small and uninteresting. They had chatted back and forth over text for a few days. She had asked him about what they were doing at the agency and had felt a strong stab of envy when he mentioned that a woman who had been her junior had been promoted to the head of the now-much-larger graphic design department. She had taken at least ten paces backwards in her career by leaving when she did. As Millie became more independent, she felt it niggle at her, forcing her to think about the wisdom of stepping back to stay home with a child.

'Leslie,' he said, standing up as she walked towards his table, 'you look radiant, but of course you always do. How are you, my love?' He had leaned forward and kissed her on the lips, making her flinch at the invasive contact, and she knew she'd made a mistake. He thought this was a reunion of some sort and she had let him think that by not calling him out when his texts got a little flirty. But she wasn't interested in a reunion with her old boyfriend. She was interested in a job, and she hadn't mentioned it to Randall because he would hate her seeing Graham. She thought it wouldn't matter unless he had something for her, and then she would deal with whatever happened later. If she had told Randall instead of keeping it from him, he would have asked her not to go and she would have listened. And she would have only been gone an hour and Millie would be here.

The meeting had only gotten more uncomfortable. They had chatted about their lives, and Millie, and Graham had asked a few questions about Randall, and then there had been a minute of silence and she had said, 'I was wondering if you had any openings. I'm looking to get back to work.'

And at the same time, he had said, 'I didn't think you were the kind of woman to do something like this, Les. Not that I mind. I've really missed you.'

They had both stopped speaking as Leslie felt the mortification of asking for a job settle on her and realised what he'd said.

'Oh,' said Graham, 'oh... so I have it wrong.' She could see that he was dealing with his own personal embarrassment and she knew that there was absolutely no chance of a job at the agency. She had been stupid to think she could go back.

'Oh well...' He had cleared his throat twice. 'Things are a bit quiet... I mean, we're busy, but not enough to... Well, you know how it goes.' He had looked down at his still, silent phone on the table. 'Um... there's my phone. I'm meeting a friend. I really have to go. Nice to see you again.' He had stood up, knocking the small table between them and tipping his coffee cup over in its saucer, the cold grey-brown dregs leaking out.

After he had gone, a waiter had presented her with the bill. He hadn't even paid for his own coffee. She was humiliated because he didn't want her and her brilliance back at work, and he was humiliated because she didn't want him back in her bed. It had been a hideous hour, and as she paid for the coffees and walked to her car, she was grateful she hadn't said anything to Randall. She just wanted to put the whole stupid incident behind her.

Now she stands up as Constable Willow hands her phone back to her. 'He's confirmed you were with him and has asked if you could give him a call. He had no idea Millie was missing.'

Leslie nods and takes her phone. She will delete Graham's number as soon as this is over. The thought makes her catch her breath. When will this be over? How will it end?

'I might just use the bathroom,' she says to no one in particular. Instead of using the downstairs bathroom, she goes upstairs to her en suite. There, she shuts and locks the door and sits on the edge of the large sunken bathtub. Millie loves this tub, loves being able to fill it with bubbles and have Leslie get in with her. Leslie rocks back and forth for a moment, her arms wrapped around herself. How will this end? A heavy pain settles in her chest.

Where are you? Where are you? Please come home, Millie Molly. Please come home.

There is a soft knock at the bathroom door and she knows it's Randall. Finally they have some time together – but now it is too late for her to tell him first. She sighs. She wanted just a little time completely alone, but this has to be dealt with now. Whatever happens, they need to be able to support each other through it. She gets up, unlocks the door and, without opening it, sits down on the edge of the tub again.

'Yes,' she says, and he comes in and sits on a white timber chair in the corner of the large bathroom.

'Why Graham?' he asks before she can say anything.

'I wanted a job,' she says, 'that's all. The website is really not doing well and I just needed...' She sighs.

'More than me and Millie,' he finishes for her. 'You needed more than me and Millie because it's not enough for you.'

He leans back, stretching out his long legs in front of him, and for a moment she understands why some of his employees are a little afraid of him, something that was whispered to her by his drunk secretary at the office summer party. It's not that he's threatening; it's more that his disappointment is so terrible to see. She knows she's let him down and she feels awful about it. She is back to blaming herself entirely for what has happened. In one afternoon, she has damaged her marriage and lost her only child. It is surely too much to survive.

'How much more can you need, Les? You have your work; you have me and Millie and Shelby. A job would just mean hours away from us all. You can't work for Graham and just do normal nine-to-five hours. I saw how you worked before we got married and had Millie. I don't know how you could go back to that, I really don't. But maybe that's what you want.' He shrugs his shoulders wearily.

'That's unfair,' she says, hurt and angry. 'Why would you say something like that?'

'Why would you go and see an old boyfriend and leave our child alone? Look what's happened.'

'What?' she yells, standing up, and then lowers her voice to a furious whisper, not wanting anyone else to hear. 'She wasn't alone, you know that. She was with your daughter, *your* daughter.'

'My daughter? So all that stuff about us being one family means nothing now? Suddenly she's only *my* daughter?' He stands up as well, leaning over her, a scowl twisting his face.

'That's not what I mean. I'm just...' She sinks down onto the side of the tub again. 'I'm sorry I saw Graham, but that's not why Millie is missing and you know it,' she says softly, even though she feels the guilt over leaving Shelby and Millie alone for hours as a heavy blanket across her shoulders. But the guilt is not hers alone. 'She should have been fine with Shelby, Randall. She should have been taken care of – or why did we ever agree to let Shelby babysit?'

'We agreed to her babysitting for short periods of time,' he says through clenched teeth. He is still standing over her and she wishes he would just move away. His aftershave, made with a touch of sandalwood, a scent she usually loves, envelops her.

'It was only a couple of hours,' she says focusing on the large cream marble tiles instead of looking at him.

'This is not Shelby's fault,' says Randall. 'It's not,' he repeats as he steps back, and she can hear something in his voice, can hear that he's been trying to convince himself of this for hours. And she understands that perhaps she can get him to agree to asking Shelby what really happened, if they can get her away from Bianca's side.

'I'm not... I'm not blaming her, but... perhaps she's keeping something from us. Something that would explain what happened.' Leslie speaks slowly, feeling herself on the edge of a precipice here. She is asking Randall to put one child ahead of the other, but at the same time... Shelby is safe and Millie is missing.

'I can't do this,' says Randall. 'I can't accuse my child of hurting her sister. I can't do that. It's not who she is.' He turns around and leaves the bathroom before Leslie can say another word. The thought has been swirling through his mind as it has been swirling through hers. His reaction proves that. She wants to cry, but her eyes are dry and scratchy.

Instead, she opens her phone and scrolls through pictures of her daughter, whose whole life has been documented, from the first smile to the first step to the first time she climbed to the top of the slide. What if she has been kidnapped? What if whoever has her is hurting her? Fury rises inside her and she stands up, her nails digging into the palm of her hand. *I will kill whoever hurts her. I will kill them.*

Even as she thinks the words, she feels herself sag, feels her body to be heavy, her thoughts useless. She has no power, no control over this situation. Her child is missing and could be anywhere at all. She walks over to the large marble vanity, where one whole wall is a mirror. Staring at herself, she can see that her brown eyes are dull, her hair a limp mess and her lips peeling and chapped. She has been biting down on them too much. She wants to smash the mirror, to throw her phone at the glass, to shatter something, to make noise and scream and shout her rage and fear.

She reaches up to her hair and tugs a few strands together, enjoying the sting of pulling them out.

Her phone vibrates and she looks down.

Your husband is not who he says he is.

It's a text message from a number she doesn't recognise.

Your husband is not who he says he is.

She sinks back down onto the side of the tub as she studies the words, her body growing chilly in the bathroom.

What could that mean? If he's not who he says he is, then who exactly is he?

CHAPTER FOURTEEN

SHELBY

She is upstairs in her room, curled up underneath the soft caramel-coloured blanket that Leslie bought for her bed. She told her mother she needed to lie down because she was feeling sick. It's not untrue. Her stomach is queasy and her head is pounding.

I'm sorry about what happened but please don't tell anyone I was there

Kiera is getting worried because she hasn't replied.

There is a soft knock at the door and her heart thumps in her chest as she quickly deletes the text with trembling fingers. She sits up. 'Yeah,' she says, and the door opens. Her mother is with the young constable. She sits up straighter, tucking the blanket tightly around her legs.

'This... policeman,' her mother says, 'would like to take a look at your phone.' Shelby can tell from the way her mother is looking at her that she wants her to refuse, but she's not going to do that. She's made sure there's nothing there now.

Her mother wants her to be difficult, wants her to make a scene. But she's too tired, too sad to do anything but agree.

'Why?' she asks, just to make sure, just to give her heart time to slow down.

'That's what I said,' her mother sneers. 'I believe this is entirely inappropriate.'

'It's okay,' says Shelby quickly. 'I don't mind.' She can see her mother working her way up into something. Her mum will happily have an argument with just about anyone. Shelby knows that she is much more like her dad in this regard. She hates arguing with anyone. It's why she let Kiera come over and why she sometimes feels like she's being pushed to do things by her friends, by her parents, by her teachers and by everyone else, pushed to do things she doesn't want to do. She admires her mother's ability to always be ready for a fight, but she just finds that idea exhausting. She's been trying, lately, to push back a little, and that's confusing everyone. But pushing back is hard, and look what it's led to, look what's happened because she tried to push back. She holds her phone out to the constable, who seems so young he could be in high school. Shelby is not looking forward to high school next year. *What if I don't get to go? What if I'm sent to jail instead? What if, what if...*

The constable smiles at her and takes the phone in its silver glitter case. She hopes he doesn't notice that her hands are shaking as she prays that Kiera does not pick right now to send another message.

Then she hunches down a little, hating that he is looking at some of the cringey stuff on there. He flicks through things quickly and hands the phone back after a few minutes. 'Thanks, Shelby. You haven't remembered anything else that could help, have you?'

Shelby shakes her head, hating that she can feel herself turning red, relief and fear colouring her face. Can he tell she's lying? How much does he know? Is he just pretending that they don't know what really happened?

'I would like to take my daughter home now,' says her mother, standing up straight so she's a little taller than the constable.

'I'll just check with Constable Dickerson,' he says, and he leaves the room.

'Pack up all your stuff,' says her mother, the decision made for Shelby, without asking her what she wants.

'Mum...' says Shelby.

'Yes?'

'Do you think it's my fault – what happened? Is it my fault?' She asks the question knowing the answer, because of course it is her fault and now she has to keep what really happened to herself and just hope with everything she has that Millie is found, although everything will be much worse then. Much worse, but also over. They won't be waiting any more. She has been, this whole time, trying to find a way to exist between knowing what happened, what she saw, what she believes to be true, and believing that she has no idea what happened to her sister. There have been moments when she has been able to convince herself that Millie is fine and she will be found soon. But the longer this goes on, the less able she is to tell herself that.

Her mum comes over to the bed and sits down. She strokes Shelby's hair. 'Of course not. When I called and you told me you'd been alone with her for over an hour, I was very upset. I was going to come over and be with you until her mother came back, but...' She waves her hand to indicate that something had stopped her.

'I wish you had,' says Shelby. But her mother hadn't come over, had instead left her alone with her little sister. Millie was not her mother's problem.

'They'll find her, I'm sure. Now pack up. Let's get you

home. We can get some takeaway Chinese.' Her mother wants this to be over, wants life back to normal, wants to pretend this day didn't happen. Shelby wants that as well.

She nods and starts to move as her mother leaves the room. She picks up her school work that she wanted to get done by Sunday night and stuffs it into her denim backpack along with some clothes she brought, although she doubts she will be doing any school work at all. It sounds like her mother doesn't care if Millie is found or not, but she knows that's not the case. Her mother believes she will be found because she believes that Millie just wandered off and is now lost. Her mother has no idea. At least she thinks her mother has no idea. She thinks and hopes that no one really knows what happened. But what if more people do know, what if more people actually know the truth?

Her phone vibrates with another text, and when she sees it's from Kiera again, relief washes over her that the constable is not here right now.

What are you going to do? Are you going to tell anyone?

Shelby thinks about what she should say, about what she *can* say, but nothing comes to mind, so she shoves her phone in her backpack. She doesn't want to talk to Kiera, not now and maybe not ever again. Kiera doesn't care about anyone but herself.

She and Kiera had not expected Millie to be so fast, had not expected her to simply dart out of the open front door and across the front garden and out the gate. 'Come back, Millie,' Shelby had screamed, even as Kiera giggled. She had taken off after her little sister and she had nearly caught up to her when Millie had turned her head and shouted, 'I hate you,' and Shelby could see she was crying and she felt so bad. Her heart ached for her. Then Millie had darted into the street, right in front of a silver car. Time had slowed down, moment by moment, as the car moved towards Millie's small body. And then—

'Ready?' asks her mother, opening her bedroom door.

'Yes,' says Shelby, 'I guess.'

'Right then. I need a glass of wine. I can't wait to put this whole day behind me.'

Shelby knows that will never happen. The day, what happened, will never be behind them. It's only just begun.

CHAPTER FIFTEEN

RUTH

She hasn't responded to my text. No one wants to hear that about a man they've chosen to have a child with. But I don't understand why she didn't immediately text me back and ask what I was talking about. I think about her lying in bed next to a man who is capable of the things he is capable of, and shudder. She probably doesn't know, or if she does, she questions whether or not she is seeing what she thinks she's seeing. Gaslighting, they call it now, making someone believe that what they think, what they believe, what they have witnessed is wrong. He was always so good at it.

You imagined it. That's not what I meant. That didn't happen the way you say it did. Is there something wrong with you? Perhaps you have a problem. You're paranoid. I really think you should see someone.

I study the text on my phone and then I go into what used to be my bedroom, just to check things out, but all is quiet; my piles in there are still neat and tidy. It is a place of safety, a place of protection. Anything in here is safe. I was safe in here, surrounded, cocooned and safe.

I sit down on my bed, the bed I used to sleep in before my

mother passed away. The mattress dips and I see myself as a little girl on this very same bed, small and perfect. I don't use this bedroom any more, but it is still a good space for me, shielded by neat collections of playing cards, all in their boxes, rolls of sticky tape in separate dispensers, white candles, large and small, unscented because I like the clean smell of a plain wax candle. In the corner there is a large collection of Christmas greeting cards, bound together with red ribbon in bundles of nine. I've never sent a Christmas card to anyone. The only people I ever spent Christmas with were my mother and grandmother and whatever man my mother was with at the time, but I like my bundles of cards, I like the optimism and hope conveyed in the messages inside. *Merry Christmas and Happy New Year*; *Wishing you a wonderful Christmas and a happy New Year*; *'Tis the season to be jolly*; *Peace on earth for all*; *Here's to a wonderful Christmas and new year for all of us.* Christmas is only a few months away and I will, once again, be alone, and that's fine, but I don't think it's fair that he will be with his wife and his little girl, who he will hurt one day. Maybe he has already begun to hurt her, and even as he appeals for help in finding her, he is hiding what he has done to her, not just today but every day. Anger at him rises inside me. He doesn't deserve a Christmas with his family, and I will make sure he doesn't get one.

I relax a little and smile, pleased with this new, fierce version of myself. 'He won't get one,' I whisper. I return to the television, waiting for updates on the missing child. It's after 5.30 now, nearly time for dinner, but my stomach won't accept food. Once I had seen him, once I was over the shock of him simply turning up in a suburban coffee shop close to where I lived, I locked myself in the house for days. I took to peering out of the front window, peeking through the curtains, expecting to see him come walking up the driveway. I don't know that if he had turned up at my door, I wouldn't have let him in. Such was his power over me when I was thirteen and fourteen that I am not sure I would be able to simply say no. I had been taught that my 'no' had little weight, that it was wrong and meant there was a problem with me.

I thought he had recognised me but was pretending not to. And then, when nothing happened, when he didn't come knocking on my door, when I accepted that he had no memory of me at all, that I had simply been a woman in a coffee shop on an ordinary day, my plan to expose him was made. It came to me one night as I stacked different colour pillowcases – six hundred of them. I understood I could use his selective memory of who mattered and who didn't to my advantage. I didn't need him to remember me until the time was right. It took me hours to fold the pillowcases, my hands moving as images of *his* hands on my body churned through me. And finally, when the pile was done and my arms ached, I knew what I had to do. I saw myself standing in front of him, my finger pointed in his direction, saying, 'Him. It was him who hurt me.'

I needed to know where he lived. I needed to know where he worked. I wondered if he was still teaching, and then felt sick at all the young girls he was busy destroying. He had to be stopped. The next day I returned to the coffee shop at around the same time as I had seen him. I drove my car so that I would be ready for whatever happened. It was easier to get out of the house with a real sense of purpose. He didn't turn up, but I didn't let that deter me. I went back again and again until the barista knew what to make as soon as he saw me. And finally, he came in. And then I watched and followed, hopping into my little Beetle – into my grandmother's lavender-scented car with my tourmaline stones for protection. He got into his car and I drove faster than I ever have, doing my best to keep up with him. He's not a teacher any more. He works in a big building with a security entrance. I watched him park and walk in, swiping a card to get the door to open. I looked up the name of the company and found him right there on their front page. Same person, different name. For two weeks I have been watching him go in and out of work.

I have never followed him to his home, because I was afraid of getting caught, but today, today of all days, I woke with a need to end this. I was going to find out where he lived and confront him. He visited the coffee shop last Saturday, on his way to get some exercise. I wondered if he would be there again today, and he was, dressed the same way, a stupid grin on his face. Last Saturday I went home after my visit to the coffee shop, but not today. Today I followed him, watched as he pulled his car over, maybe to take a call, and then off he drove again, my little yellow Beetle keeping up nicely. I could never have imagined what I would see then. Perhaps it is a good thing I was there to see, to witness. Perhaps not.

I can't watch the news again; can't see the mother's despair and his fake grief. The mother must be suffering terribly. But if she will just respond, I can tell her what she needs to know.

My phone remains annoyingly silent. I want her to ask what I mean and then I can explain about him. Once I've done that, she will have all the information she needs. I don't know why she hasn't even asked me who I am.

Maybe she thinks the text is a joke? I nod my head, yes, that's what it is. She doesn't believe me. She will need more evidence. I go to the kitchen and grab my laptop and type his real name into Google. It's not his name any more. He changed it when he left, ran, bolted. He changed it and became someone else, and no one has ever thought to check that he's not who he says he is – not at all.

CHAPTER SIXTEEN

LESLIE

6.00 p.m.

In the kitchen, Leslie stands by the kettle, clicking it on, waiting for it to boil and switch off only to click it on again. She cannot seem to move from the spot she is standing in. It's after 6 p.m. and she can hear the drone of the television from the living room. The amber alert for Millie is being repeated in every news break. The newsreader's voice drops a tone whenever she says 'amber alert', indicating to those listening that this is now very, very serious. Leslie has seen these alerts before and always felt the tingle of worry that every mother feels, but she also knows that they are usually quickly followed by news that the missing child or children have been located. That's what she's hoping for now, that someone, somewhere has seen something and Millie will be found and brought home, that she hasn't been taken. *Please God, don't let someone have taken her, don't let her be in the hands of a stranger.*

On Saturday nights, Millie gets to choose what she wants for dinner. She always picks Leslie's home-made pizza, even though she pretends to really think about what she might like. If

Randall is with them in the kitchen when she is choosing what to eat, he will turn it into a game. 'I think you want a burger,' he will begin.

'Nope,' Millie will smile.

'I think you want a flower from the garden.'

'Nope, silly Daddy. I can't eat flowers. I'm a person.'

'I think you want cabbage soup.'

'No, yuck, come on, Daddy, choose something better.'

'I think you want bug stew.'

'Ew, yuck, yuck,' Millie inevitably giggles. 'I want pizza, Mum's pizza.'

Leslie thinks about the text again. How can he not be who she thinks he is? He is the head of a tech company and he's frequently in the business pages giving his advice on where things are going in the tech world. Lately he has started going into schools to lecture students on running a business. 'Apparently I'm still a natural teacher,' he told her after the first time. 'The kids were really eager to hear what I had to say, and I might think about mentoring some of them. Girls especially need to be encouraged to get into computing.' Before he sold his software program, he had been a casual teacher – a job with no benefits or sick pay and no guarantee of work, but with plenty of time for him to work on his program. It had driven Bianca mad. 'She thought it was a waste of my degree,' Randall had told Leslie, and Leslie could see how easy it would have been to be frustrated with Randall, to need him to do something else with his life, to become a proper provider.

If he wasn't who he said he was, someone would know, wouldn't they? Someone would have found out and exposed him.

But maybe that's exactly what's going to happen. Maybe Millie has been taken because of something Randall has done or because of who he is. Who is he? Leslie wraps her arms around herself. The sound from the television is starting to drive her mad. She thinks about her plan with Randall this morning for pizza and a bottle of wine, for a movie on Netflix, for something they did virtually every Saturday night. Will there ever be another Saturday night like that again?

Trevor comes into the kitchen. 'Is there anything I can do to help, Leslie?' he asks.

The question makes Leslie want to explode. It has been asked so many times in the last few hours by so many different people, and the only answer she wants to give is 'Find my daughter.'

She breathes in and turns from her position at the kettle to face him. 'No thank you, Trevor, everyone's doing... what they can.' There is tension in her neck and jaw as she says this, making sure to be polite, because no one likes a rude mother of a missing child. The woman who complimented her on her home has left, and Leslie is sure that she was angry about the way she behaved.

'I imagine the waiting is driving you insane,' he says. 'Sorry about the stupid question. I know you just want her found.'

'Yes,' she agrees, pleased to have someone say this aloud. 'I just... I can't believe they haven't found her already.' Her eyes fill with tears and she blinks rapidly to stop them falling. If she starts, if she lets go, there will be no stopping.

Trevor nods his understanding. She doesn't know him very well, but he seems a nice person. He's only been married to Bianca for six months, and even though Leslie had her doubts about the relationship, she has had the opportunity to watch them together once or twice and she believes that they are right for each other.

Randall was defeated by Bianca's large personality, and over the years of their marriage he found himself defeated by her wants and needs. He always looks apologetic in her company and Leslie knows this is because Bianca told him over and again that he was failing at being a husband and father, at being a provider. But she can see that Trevor has a different approach. Instead of allowing Bianca's jabs to land and hurt, he smiles and shrugs his shoulders and then goes on doing what he wants to do. And while Leslie would expect Bianca to find this maddening, she seems to be fine with it. Maybe that was all that was needed – for her barbs to be ignored. Leslie wishes she could take the same approach, but Bianca makes her feels inadequate, and while she counsels her husband to ignore his ex-wife, she finds it impossible to do the same.

The kettle clicks off again, and because Trevor is watching her, she lifts it up and pours the boiled water into the cup she has placed there. As the water touches the tea bag and turns dark and murky, she thinks about the lake at the park, and she keeps pouring, the water spreading across the counter, until Trevor grabs the kettle. 'Oops,' he says, and he quickly grabs a tea towel to clean up the spill.

She shakes her head as she watches him, feeling slightly bad for thinking negatively about Bianca. There must be something nice about the woman. She has, after all, managed to raise Shelby and keep her safe. At least she can say she has done the one thing that every mother is supposed to do.

It has always been important to Randall to maintain a good relationship with his ex-wife for Shelby's sake, and so when Bianca married Trevor, he asked Leslie to invite the two of them over for dinner.

'She never even looks at me, Randall. I really don't want her in my house,' Leslie had said at the time.

'I know, but Shelby is getting older and I want her to know that all the adults in her life are at least cordial with each other. I don't want a teenage daughter who thinks she can pit us against each other. It's hard enough to be a pre-teen girl these days without having to deal with divorced parents and a new sibling.' And Leslie had felt that, somehow, she was being criticised, even though she knew it was not the case.

She had agreed to the dinner, fretting over what to cook for days. Bianca and Trevor had arrived bearing wine and chocolates and Bianca had nodded in her direction, but then she had spent the whole night looking at and talking to Shelby and Randall and making a particular effort to not finish her food, twisting her mouth while eating as though tasting something awful. Trevor had seen what was happening and Leslie knows that because he made sure to speak to her, to ask her about her work and about Millie, who was upstairs asleep. He sold insurance, which he admitted was mostly boring and time-consuming, but he managed to make her laugh with stories of strange clients, like the man who wanted to insure his dead wife's ashes.

'They will find her, Leslie, I'm sure of it,' he says now, dragging her from her thoughts.

'Where could she be?' she asks, as though he might have the answer.

'Maybe...' he begins.

'Maybe?'

He shrugs his shoulders. 'I have no idea. Do you think it's possible she and Shelby had a fight about something?'

'I don't know.' Leslie shakes her head, because she has been thinking of this possibility all along. She and Trevor are not Shelby's biological parents, and so it feels underhand to be discussing her in this way. Neither Randall nor Bianca wants to hear a word said against their child, which is understandable. But someone has to say something, because it's possible; no one wants to think it or acknowledge it, but it is completely possible.

There have been times when Shelby's patience with her little sister wears thin and she yells at her to go away, and Millie is always devastated when this happens. Being irritated by your little sister, wanting some space and sometimes shouting to make your point is normal in a sibling relationship, and maybe that's what happened today. But Leslie has no idea if Millie would have been so upset by Shelby yelling at her that she actually ran away – and why she has not returned, if this was the case. Or perhaps something else happened, something that Shelby knows she will be blamed for, something that she is hiding.

'I might go out and join the searchers again,' says Trevor. 'I just need to duck home and get a warm jacket.'

'Thank you,' smiles Leslie, and then she wipes her eyes because a smile feels so very wrong.

He turns to leave.

'Um, Trevor,' she says, suddenly feeling that she can trust this man. 'Can I ask you something?'

'Sure,' he says.

She pulls her phone out of her pocket and shows him the text message. She obviously can't show it to Randall, and right now there is no one else here for her to talk to. 'Do you think I should show this to the police?'

He reads the message and frowns. 'When did you get that?' he asks.

'About half an hour ago. I don't know what to do about it.'

'I think,' he says slowly, 'that you should definitely show the police. It's odd that you've been contacted like this and it may be that... Well, it's not for me to say. I just think you should show them.'

His certainty alarms Leslie. At that moment, Constable Dickerson walks into the kitchen. Trevor nods at her and moves away and then out of the kitchen, leaving them alone.

The constable looks at the kettle and rubs his hands together, a sympathetic smile crossing his face. 'I think we're going to let Shelby go home with her mother,' he says. 'We're sending one of our other constables to her house in case she remembers anything over the next few hours, but I just wanted to let you know.'

'Okay,' says Leslie, and he turns to go but she reaches out and touches the sleeve of his uniform. 'I need to show you this,' and then she turns her phone to the policeman, watches as he reads it slowly, mouthing the words.

'Who's it from?' he asks.

Leslie feels frustration bubble up inside her. 'I don't know, that's why I'm showing it to you.'

'Do *you* think your husband is not who he appears to be?' he asks, his face a mask of patience.

'No, I...' Leslie stops speaking, her cheeks burning with humiliation.

'Look,' says Constable Dickerson softly, 'it's probably just a troll, you know, someone entertaining themselves with your... misery. I'm surprised you haven't had more messages. You have a website and your number is easily found. Give the number to Constable Willow and he can add it to the list of numbers to check. There have been a lot of calls and we will get to every one of them. In the meantime, maybe you should try and get some rest.'

Leslie feels a wave of fury surge through her. She has shown him something that might be connected with her missing child and he has done the equivalent of patting her hand and saying, 'There, there, dear. Don't worry your pretty head over it.'

'My child,' she says, her back teeth clamped together so the words emerge in a strangled hiss, 'my baby girl is out there, lost or with someone. It's nearly dark and it's cold and she's not here, not here in my home where she should be, and you want me to get some rest? What kind of a person could rest?'

The constable raises his hands. 'I understand, Leslie, believe me I understand. We'll look into it. We will. We just have a lot of stuff to go through right now. You don't know how many calls we're getting. Hundreds and hundreds have come through to Crime Stoppers. There are so many people who think they know something or who want to pretend they know something. One woman called to tell us that you and Randall are part of a satanic cult and that you've sacrificed your child and she has proof.'

'That's ridiculous and disgusting,' screams Leslie, failing to hold back her tears or her anger.

'I know, I know...' says the constable soothingly.

'Hey, hey, Les, what's going on?' asks Randall, darting into the kitchen and immediately coming to her side. He puts his arms around her, holding her tightly.

'It's just...' She stops crying and shoves her phone into her pocket as she feels herself sag against him. Obviously it's just a troll. Of course it's not a clue or a way to get her little girl back. She feels stupid and completely exhausted. *Millie Molly, where are you? Where are you?*

'Your wife received a strange message on her phone,' says the constable. 'I probably should have warned you about the possibility of those coming in.'

'Yes,' says Leslie, needing to try and convince him that this is something, 'but what if it's from the...' The word 'kidnapper' feels wrong to say. Kidnapping is something that happens in the movies. She pulls her phone out of her pocket again, wanting him to look at the message, to really see the message.

'Anyone who means to contact you about your daughter will let you know they have her first,' says Constable Dickerson. 'That's been our experience. A message like the one you've received is just meant to confuse and hurt you. We've seen it many times. I've worked two actual kidnappings in my time and I can tell you that the first thing they did was to make sure we understood they had the child. And each time we recovered the child safe and well. Please know that we are doing absolutely everything we can to find your daughter. I understand how awful this is, but we are doing everything possible.'

'What message?' asks Randall. 'Show me the message.' He grabs for the phone and Leslie steps back, shocked at the slightly desperate move. He raises his hands in apology. 'Sorry, can you show me?' he says, gritting his teeth.

Leslie gives him her phone and watches a frown of concern appear on his face as he reads it.

'Do you have any idea who it could be from?' she asks him.

He shakes his head. 'No.' He hands the phone back to her. 'You're not actually worried about that, are you? The constable is right. It's obviously just some troll.' A dry laugh escapes. 'If I'm not who you think I am, then who *am* I, Les?'

Leslie shakes her head. She doesn't have the answer to that question.

'Maybe I should just call the number and see who answers,' says Leslie.

'Don't do that, Les,' says Randall quickly. 'It could be a scam of some sort, designed to hack into your phone. Just let the police handle it.'

'Perhaps you need to have a bit of a rest,' says the constable once more, and Leslie shrugs her shoulders and leaves the kitchen, defeated by everyone's desire for her to be quiet and unseen so they can get on with what they have to do.

Randall follows her upstairs in silence, and she has the feeling that he is making sure she does go to their bedroom.

'I'm fine. You don't need to come with me,' she says, because if she's going to lie down on her bed, she wants to be alone. She has not given the number to Constable Willow, but what does it matter? The explanations of a troll or a scammer trying their luck are probably more logical than her idea of someone contacting her because they know something that may help. The constable is right about it being an odd message for someone to send if they do have Millie.

Instead of going back downstairs, Randall follows her into the room and then shuts the door behind him.

She sighs and climbs onto the bed, running her hand over

the soft pale green silk of the duvet and then propping a pillow behind her, her phone clutched in her hand.

She wishes she could close her eyes and sleep, only opening them to news that her daughter has been found. Her joints ache with exhaustion. Randall stands next to the bed, his hands in his pockets, studying her. His lips move slightly as though he wants to say something to her but is unsure of how to say it. But she doesn't want to speak to him, not now. She doesn't want to speak to anyone.

'You can leave. I'm fine,' she says.

'Are you? You know, even before this... before today, you've been kind of strange.' One hand moves to his head and smooths down his curls and then returns to his pocket. He fidgets when he is having uncomfortable conversations.

'What are you talking about, Randall?'

'I don't know.' He takes his glasses off and cleans them on his shirt. 'Like pulling away or something, I don't know, and then you go and see Graham... I don't know, Les. I feel like there's something up with you.' He keeps cleaning his glasses so he doesn't have to look at her. He hates confrontation and she can see that he's been working his way up to saying this to her for some time.

'Now is not the time, not the time at all,' she says, and she looks at the window, staring at a street light, finding it impossible to believe that it's dark and her child is not home.

'Why would someone say you're not who you say you are?' she asks, instead of letting the conversation go any further.

Randall returns his glasses to his face. 'Maybe none of us are who we say we are,' he says, and then he leaves the bedroom, closing the door with a soft click.

CHAPTER SEVENTEEN
SHELBY

In the car on the way home, her mother is silent. Trevor has stayed to help look for Millie. It seems impossible that they haven't found her already. Someone knows where she is. Someone, not Shelby. Shelby has no idea where she is, but she knows what will happen if she says something, anything.

'What will happen if they never find her?' she says to her mother.

'I don't know. But I don't want you to think about this anymore tonight. You need to get some rest.' Her mother's eyes are focused on the road ahead, street lights blending into a whizzing yellow as she drives. Shelby can feel they would both like to say more, to talk more, but there is too much to say and so they are silent. Her mother has been so much happier over these last few months, almost content in some moments. Shelby had grown used to her turning every situation into a reason to blame her dad for something. It was more than just about the money; it was the idea that he had someone in his life and that they had another child. 'I would have liked a second child,' her mum had told Shelby when Millie was born. 'But I had to work so your father could take time to concentrate on his program, and now look where I am.'

'Maybe now that you're married again you can have another baby,' Shelby had suggested a few months ago.

'I'm too old,' her mum replied. 'Your father got himself a younger model so he could have another child.'

Trevor makes her mother happier than she's ever been, but there is always something simmering beneath the surface, something strange in the way her mother looks at the world, like she can't see anyone except herself. But that's not something Shelby would ever say to anyone. Sometimes she thinks that maybe *she's* the problem. If not for her, her mother would have had a much easier life. She has tried so hard to be good and to achieve at school so she can make her mum happy, but she's never managed it for very long.

'Who cares what she thinks?' Kiera told her when Shelby confessed that she sometimes wondered if her mother regretted having her. 'All mothers are just...' She waved her hand dismissively, and that made Shelby feel much better.

But she still wants her mother to be happy, to stay happy.

'None of this is your fault,' her mother says again now. 'It's *her* fault for leaving you alone with a child who didn't listen.' Her mum's hands are on the steering wheel in the exact position they should be, and she is sitting up straight and tall in her seat.

'What do you mean, didn't listen?'

'Well, she ran away, didn't she? That's not listening. She should have known better.' Her mother nods her head, agreeing with herself. 'She ran away, the selfish little girl. She's too young to know the effect it will have on people, of course, but still... It's because she's so spoilt. She doesn't know how to behave.'

'That's not true,' whispers Shelby. 'Millie is very good and she always listens.'

'Well, maybe that's what you think, but you don't live there all the time, thank God. You have no idea what goes on when you're not there.'

Shelby stares down at her phone, which she has switched off, watching the street lights bounce off the black screen. It's so hard to be the person between her mother and father. She feels like it's betraying her mother to love Millie and Leslie, and she has tried hard not to, but Millie is… Millie was…

'What would you do if it was me? How would you feel?' she asks, after a few silent minutes.

Her mother doesn't like Leslie, but not for any particular reason, just because she is with Shelby's father now that he's rich, and Shelby wonders if she has any sympathy for what Leslie is going through. She wishes she could just tell her everything, but the truth will be too much. Before Bianca met Trevor, when it was just Shelby and her mum, alone in an apartment, Shelby used to worry about her all the time. Whenever she went over to her father's house, she used to think about how lonely her mother was with just the television for company. Bianca doesn't have a lot of friends and Shelby knows that this is because she comes across as quite rude and abrupt, but mostly she's just sad and angry that her life didn't work out the way she wanted it to. 'I could have done so much more than just get a job as an assistant,' she has told Shelby. 'If your father had gotten himself a proper job when you were younger, I could have returned to school to study psychology. But my dreams had to be put on hold and now it's too late.'

Shelby isn't sure her mum would make a good psychologist. At school they have a psychologist who comes on Tuesdays, and she's sweet and kind and smiles at everyone. She seems like the sort of person who would be easy to speak to, whereas Shelby is scared to speak to her mother, to really speak to her about what happened. She's had two sessions with the school psychologist, a woman named Fran, and because Fran is so nice and approachable, Shelby has almost, almost allowed herself to share some of the things that have been bothering her. But she is smarter than that. Her mother and father keep saying that she can tell them what's upsetting her and that they can sort it out, but she knows that's not possible. They've sent her to the psychologist because they are both hoping that Fran will fix her, turn her back into good, obedient Shelby, but that can't happen, because she is weighed down with secrets.

And now she is even heavier with things she is not telling anyone, and added to that is the lie that Millie ran away, although technically she *did* run away, she did.

'How would you feel, Mum?' she asks again, because her mother hasn't replied.

Her mother glances at her quickly. 'I would feel... I would be absolutely broken, of course, Shelby – you know that. Any mother in this situation is just beside herself with worry.'

'If you knew something that would help, would you tell? I mean, even if it would get other people into trouble, would you tell?'

They are home, and her mother pulls the car into the driveway, switching off the engine and sitting in silence in the cooling car. She doesn't look at Shelby but rather down at her nails, studying them in the low light.

'You don't know anything that could help, Shelby. She ran away. That's what happened. You've explained all of that to the police and they're searching everywhere. She's probably a little scared and hiding somewhere, just hiding. She's probably in that big park. It's large and it would be difficult to find a small child there. It's only been a few hours. I know it seems like a long time, but it's only a few hours and they will find her soon.' Her mother sounds completely certain, as though she knows that this is the absolute truth, but Shelby thinks it's just wishful thinking on her part.

'It's getting colder and she didn't have her jacket. She hates to be cold and she's scared of the dark. She's only three, Mum.'

'I know that, Shelby.' Her mother shakes her head and bites down on her lip. 'Don't you think I know that?'

Shelby opens the car door and gets out. The house where her mother lives needs a lot of work. She and Trevor bought it a few months before they got married and Trevor told her that they would do it up together. It's got three bedrooms and a wraparound porch that used to sag and dip but is now gleaming polished wood. It will be a nice place to sit in the summer. Trevor works on some part of the house every weekend. Sometimes her mum helps, and if they are working together, Shelby can see that Trevor makes her mother very happy. They talk and laugh together all the time. Her mother is finally okay after all her years of being angry and sad. It would be nice if that happiness extended to Shelby's father, but if she even mentions anything she has done with Leslie and her dad, her mother is instantly angry with the world. She tries not to talk about things that she does at her father's house when she is home with her mother, and the same thing with her father – even though she knows she could tell him about her life with her mother and Trevor and he wouldn't mind. She gets the feeling that she needs to protect both families. She's the only link between them and she needs to be careful what she shares. It's very tiring. Or at least it was, because now that this has happened, everything is going to have to be shared. She can feel that. How can she keep secrets from her mother now?

Shelby doesn't like being in this house on the weekend, where her dreams fill up with the sounds of hammers and chainsaws. She prefers it at her father's house, where a Saturday morning is the smell of pancakes and Millie standing in her doorway, whispering but not really whispering, 'Are you waked up yet, Shelby?'

This morning she had been resentful about having to babysit Millie. Now she wonders if she will ever get the chance to take care of her little sister again.

CHAPTER EIGHTEEN

RUTH

It takes me an hour of searching before I find exactly what I'm looking for, and that's because I'm not actually sure what I *am* looking for. I just know it's something, something that I can show this mother, this sad mother of a missing little girl, so that she knows exactly who she is married to, exactly who she has in her bed at night and who she chose to procreate with. She needs to know. When I was a teenager, I tried to tell my mother, to explain that she had it all wrong and that Touchy Tony was even worse than she knew, but he explained it all away, and no matter what I said, she wouldn't believe me. It's not that I haven't looked him up before. I have, but mostly on Facebook, and he's changed his name so obviously I was never going to find anything. He still doesn't have a Facebook profile, but that's probably because he's worried his past will come back to get him. Last year, a young woman from a private school started a website that asked other girls to talk about all the times they had experienced sexual assault in any form. I remember reading through the accounts, feeling the anguish in their words and wanting desperately to write my own story. But even though I could see that the site was a safe space, a space where no matter what I wrote, I would be acknowledged, I still didn't do it. What if they tell me I'm lying? I thought. What if he somehow reads it and accuses me of libel? What if someone says I'm making all of this up? He still has a hold over me, still after all these years. But not for long.

I click through page after page on the internet and eventually feel my eyes begin to burn a little. It's after 7 p.m. and I want to leave this and read a book or something, but I can't, of course. I have to see it through. And then finally, I find what I need. Click through enough pages on the internet and everyone's past is revealed. Nothing stays hidden any more.

It's an article from a small local newspaper. I check the date and calculate that it was seven years after he removed himself from my life. He still had the same name. Whatever happened at his next school must have led him to change it.

I read the words slowly, thinking them through. They don't tell anyone anything unless you knew about him already. If you knew about him already, then it's easy to read between the lines, easy to read the terse message from the school principal as something other than a fond goodbye. But if you don't know about him, because you have been tricked, conned, deceived by him, then it just seems like a brief article wishing a teacher leaving a school the best of luck for the future. What it does have, what makes it the something I have been searching for, is the picture of him smiling at the camera as he talks to a group of students, pleased with himself. He was always very pleased with himself.

The photograph is a little grainy, and many years old, but it's obviously him. He hasn't changed much over the years. I recognised him right away and I know that his wife will as well.

I save the link and then I go searching for her email address. She didn't respond to my text but maybe she will respond to an email. I look for her Facebook profile as well, but can't seem to find it. Her work email will have to do. I compose a message slowly, painstakingly, deleting and retyping the few words over and again. But I don't send it. One piece of advice my mother gave me – one of the only really good pieces of advice – was to wait before I did something that couldn't be undone. I need to think about what I'm doing, about the consequences of sending her the message. She will contact me, I'm sure of it, and then I will be pulled from my safe space out into the world, into the glare of the public, and I will have to tell what happened to me and I will have to explain what I've done. I'm not sure I'm ready for that. My heart quickens at the thought of having to leave this space, of being looked at, of being seen. Can I do it?

I am hungry for something to eat and I make myself a dinner of chicken soup and toast. While I wait for the soup to heat, I visit my old childhood bedroom twice more, but nothing has changed in there. Everything is still neat and safe, and even if I do this, I will always have my bedroom, my home to come back to. I hope. I quickly knock over a pile of packs of playing cards and stack them up again. I do it three times so that I return to calm, so that I can think straight.

In the kitchen, I eat my soup slowly, working through the consequences of sending the article. Truthfully, I believe that I sent such a cryptic message in the first place because I wasn't entirely sure I was ready for what will happen. But I can't wait any longer. I have a duty to this little girl. I have a duty to change the way her life plays out, because when she returns home, he cannot be there. I imagine his sneaky, clever hands and the way he would touch me right in front of other people without batting an eye, the way other people would see and not see.

I sit down in front of my computer, my finger over the 'enter' button, the little arrow over the word 'send'. I take a deep breath. I hit the button and it's gone. Too late to rethink things now.

As I make myself a cup of tea, I think again about calling the police. I could end this all right now – point the finger, tell them what happened – but I have no desire to have the spotlight cast on me just yet, and when the little girl is found, when she does get to return home, I need to know that he will no longer be there. That's what I'm waiting for. The mother will read the article and contact me, and then I will tell her everything.

'But I don't understand,' I imagine her saying, and then I explain so that she does.

I once saw a television show where a lawyer pressured a man to testify against a murderer by saying, 'You wouldn't want this to happen to anyone else, would you?' I wouldn't want what happened to me to happen to any other young girl, and yet I have let it happen, for decades, I'm sure. I have allowed him to go on hurting other little girls because I allowed myself to be silenced.

In the living room I walk over to my pile of blue books, chosen because blue is a calming colour. They are all hardcover, some stippled and rough, some smooth and sleek, some soft with age. I push at the pile until it falls over, and I begin my stacking. She will contact me soon. I'm sure of it.

CHAPTER NINETEEN

LESLIE

8.00 p.m.

Leslie is in her bedroom, standing at the window, her hands wrapped in the dove-grey silk curtains, crushing the material as she absent-mindedly scrunches it. She has been so careful with the expensive fabric, careful to only touch it with clean hands, to pull gently to open the curtains in the morning to let the light in, to make sure Millie doesn't decide they are somewhere to hide, wrapping herself in the soft fabric. But what does it matter if the fabric is crushed and creased, oily with the sweat from her hands?

The curtains are complemented by a carpet that goes by the colour 'ash', thick pile that is wonderful to sink your toes into at the end of a long day. Everything in the room matches, and she often hears Randall sigh as he walks in, peace descending as he enters the space.

There is a full moon tonight, casting an eerie glow over the street, shadowing the stars. Leslie is thinking of Millie watching the sunset and waiting for the stars to appear – if she's not distracted by a game or the television. She is repeating a little rhyme she and Millie sing together often. 'Star light, star bright, first star I see tonight. I wish I may, I wish I might, have this wish I wish tonight.' She is whispering the words, and each time she gets to the end, she whispers her daughter's name and makes a wish that she will be here soon, back in her bedroom, where she has a pink canopy bed and a soft cuddly unicorn to sleep with.

Leslie is alone and is supposed to be resting, but her conversation with Randall has made her edgy. Is he hiding something, something that would explain what happened here today? Is he, perhaps, hiding something about Shelby? Hiding it from Leslie, hiding it from himself? Her back is stiff, aching with tension, but to rest would be to give in, give up. She is watching, waiting for her child to return, waiting for one of the searchers to turn up with Millie in their arms, waiting for a police car to screech into the driveway with her in the back. She is waiting. She keeps playing out the day in her head, trying to make it end differently. If she had told Graham that it would be better to meet on a school day, when Millie was safely in class under the watchful eye of Mr Jackson, her genial pre-school teacher, she would not be here. If she hadn't gotten to the checkout and then realised she had forgotten tomatoes and had to turn around and go and get them, losing her place in line, she wouldn't be here. If she had just taken Millie with her and let the child have a chocolate milkshake while she talked to Graham, she wouldn't be here. There are so many ways she could have changed this day. But she's not the first mother to ask a twelve-year-old to babysit or to take too long at the grocery store. She's not even the first mother to have a slightly clandestine meeting with someone, however innocent it was. There are parents who let their children play in the street, who ignore them in favour of drugs and alcohol, who neglect or beat them, and they rarely suffer a blow from the hand of fate. Why her? Why now? Why this little girl, who is only sweetness and light and a joy to have in the world?

There is a knock at her bedroom door, and she sighs, because she has no energy for another strained conversation with anyone.

'Come in,' she calls.

Constable Dickerson comes into the room, followed by Constable Willow and Randall, and Leslie knows, absolutely knows, that they've found her. Her heart lifts, and then immediately she is terrified, because they are not joyous, are not smiling. Instead, all three men look downcast, awkward, the bearers of bad news.

'What?' she asks urgently. 'What?'

'We think we have a credible lead, and I wanted to let you know. We have constables from the local area en route to check it out.' Constable Dickerson's voice is soft, but there is something that Leslie hears. Hope? Fear? Despair?

'Which area?' asks Randall.

'West Hills, it's about forty minutes from here. Do you know it?'

'That's, um...' Randall hesitates, 'close to where I play golf.'

The constable gives him a tight smile, and Leslie watches Constable Willow write something down in his little notebook. Her stomach is queasy.

'Right, so while we wait, I wanted to play you the recording of the call, just in case you recognise the woman's voice.'

'But shouldn't we go there?' asks Leslie, looking around the room to locate her jacket. 'Let's just go there.'

'Local police are nearly there, Leslie. There's no point unless they find something, and we're not completely sure of what they will find. Can you please just listen to the recording?'

But Leslie is not ready to give up on rushing to the car. 'How long will it take them to get there? When will they call us? Will they call as soon as they have her?' She fires questions at the constable, unable to stop herself.

'We will have video feed as they arrive so you can identify if it's Millie, but please, can you listen to the call?'

Leslie holds back her other questions as she folds her arms and steps away from Randall slightly. *Close to where I play golf. Your husband is not who he says he is.*

Her whole body is humming with tension. Randall takes off his glasses and cleans them while the constable starts the recording on his phone: a burst of static, loud in the silent room, and then a cheery female voice begins, 'Hello, Crime Stoppers, can I help?'

A woman's voice that immediately identifies her as older is heard next. 'Well, yes, you can, thank you. I've just never seen people in that house, you see. I mean, it's never had a for sale sign, nothing. I was at my daughter's house for the week in Queensland, at my Marie's house, and I only got back today.'

'Yes, ma'am, and which house is this?'

'It's the one next door, next door to me, and I live at 270 Clementine Road, West Hills, near that big golf course that they should never have been allowed to build if you ask me. Too much traffic.'

'Right, and you say there are people in the house next door?'

'Well, yes. I got back and I was just unpacking and doing a wash – you know, you always have things to wash when you travel, don't you? Even though my Marie insisted on doing laundry for me every day. She knows I like my things clean.'

'Yes, and you said there were people in the house next door?' Leslie can hear that the woman who has answered the phone at Crime Stoppers is trying for patience. She can imagine that a lot of lonely people call the service just for a chat. But this is obviously not just a chat.

'Well,' sniffs the caller, clearly a little miffed at being directed. 'As I was saying, I was doing a wash and I had the news on, and I saw the story about that poor little mite – you know, the missing little girl, such a pretty thing. And I thought how sad her mum must be, and then wouldn't you know, I hear a sound from outside my bedroom window and I go to look, because you do, don't you? There's a cat from one street over that likes to visit sometimes and I hoped it was him, because I give him a saucer of milk and he likes that, and I was wondering if I had fresh milk, but it wasn't the cat.'

'No, and what did you see?' asks the other woman, her voice a touch more strident.

'Well, I saw that there was someone in the house next door. My bedroom window looks straight into the window of one of the bedrooms in that house, and for the last year, since Betty moved out, it's been empty, so I knew it hadn't sold. I saw someone, a man I think, holding a little girl who was just kind of slumped in his arms, and I noticed that she had long black hair just like the missing one on the television, and I saw that the man was wearing a kind of pink shirt, and then he turned and saw me and just ran out of the room, bolted as if he'd been caught. Well, no one is supposed to live there, you see, so I thought, that's odd, and I was going to go and knock on the door, but then I thought, well, I'm sure I didn't really see that. It was probably just because I was tired. So I went to look again and the room was as empty as it's ever been. I had a little nap after that, but now I've watched the news again and she's still missing and I thought, well, what if it is her?'

'Right, and what time was this?'

'It was a while ago. I think I saw the man at around one o'clock or maybe it was later this afternoon. I called my Marie to ask what I should do, and after I told her the story, she told me not to go next door under any circumstances but to ring the police, and I'd seen the Crime Stoppers number on the television screen, you know, like at the bottom, so I called you instead. It's the missing little girl. I just know it is.'

'Thank you, ma'am, and can you just confirm your address for me? We'll be sending someone out right away.'

'Right away... Goodness, I should have called this afternoon. She was just slumped in his arms, not like a sleeping child at all. I mean, she looked... and I hate to say this, but she looked like she was... dead.'

'We're sending someone over now. Could you just confirm your address for me?'

Constable Dickerson stops the recording. 'Right, do you recognise her voice at all? Do you have any idea of where that address is?'

'No,' says Randall quickly, but Leslie just shakes her head. She has been inching away from Randall bit by bit as they were listening to the call, inching away as she hears what the woman says. *Close to where I play golf... pink shirt. Your husband is not who he says he is.*

How much does she really know about Randall? She's only known him for five years. He had a whole other life with a wife and a child before he met her. He had a different job, or at least he had a lot of different jobs. He did some teaching to, as he put it, keep the wolf from the door, and he worked in the Apple Store on weekends to supplement his teaching income, angering Bianca, who wanted him to use his computer science degree to get a better and more high-paying job. But he'd been dedicated to getting his software program done, oblivious to the needs of his family. Leslie can see why Bianca would have told him to give up. She's had to work since Shelby was little so that they could pay the mortgage and whatever else they needed as a family.

Constable Dickerson's phone rings. 'Dickerson,' he says. 'Right, good. Thanks.' He turns the phone to face them so they can see. 'Here we go, they're at the house.'

It's a disorienting video to watch, and Leslie realises that it must be because one of the police officers is holding a phone to film so they can see if it's Millie. Her heart is beating loudly in her ears and she wraps her arms tightly around herself as they watch a hand knock on a door with chipped white paint and a rusted circle door knocker.

And then they watch the door open, watch it slowly open…

CHAPTER TWENTY

SHELBY

She wakes up on her bed, unsure how she managed to doze off. Her bedside clock tells her it's after 9 p.m. She remembers that Millie is missing. She feels sick as she imagines her cold and crying, and then she has to get up and rush to the bathroom, her bladder nearly bursting, and she thinks that Millie may not be cold or crying. Millie may be dead. Of course she's dead. They would have found her otherwise.

There is a policewoman sitting in the living room on the battered leather sofa. She is quite young, with bouncy brown hair tied into a ponytail and nice green eyes. She keeps coming to the bedroom to ask Shelby if she's remembered anything else and if she's okay, which seems to Shelby a stupid question. How on earth can she be okay? Shelby has kept shaking her head, but she doesn't know how much longer she can hold out for. The policewoman, who told them to call her Kate, knows something. Shelby is sure of it.

She leaves the bathroom, meaning to return to her bedroom, because there is no way she can go and sit in the living room with the eagle-eyed policewoman. She has a feeling she will just tell her everything without wanting to. Her room here isn't as big as her room at her father's house, but she's never minded that. Her mother let her paint one wall in a bright greeny blue, and she's got a duvet and blanket to match that colour. The door needs to be left open, because Kate said, 'Just leave it a little open, if you don't mind. That way if I need anything I can look and see if you're sleeping.' It was meant to sound nice, but Shelby also knows that it's because the policewoman wants to be able to hear if she does anything suspicious.

She holds her phone as she stands by her bedroom door and clicks it on, hoping Kate won't pick now to come and check on her.

The first text is one that she has been expecting, so it doesn't even surprise her, even though her heart rate gets faster and she feels sweat under her arms. It doesn't shock her, because the one thing she knows for sure is that no matter how much someone is supposed to love you, or how much they say they're your friend, or how much they say they care, everyone is only looking out for themselves. It's just a number, because she has never wanted to give the sender a name.

You need to keep quiet about this, she reads, and she immediately deletes the message and clicks off her phone. She can't do this anymore. She just can't.

CHAPTER TWENTY-ONE

RUTH

I look at my watch. It's nearly 9 p.m. Why hasn't she responded? Surely she's looked at it by now. Although maybe not. I sent it to her work email. Maybe she's not checking her work email. I want to turn on the news, but I know if I see him standing next to her, I will not be able to function. I can already feel the panic attack coming.

I am getting jittery now. I thought it would all be over and I could return to my solitary, safe life, knowing that I had done the right thing. *Have* I done the right thing? Will exposing him make up for what happened to me and to his little girl?

I look at my computer again, refreshing my inbox, but there's nothing. I get up and go to my childhood bedroom. I have a collection of sixty teddy bears. I collect them from charity shops, knowing that each one was probably well loved at some point. Of all the stores I force myself to go into, charity shops are the easiest for me. They are often filled with strange people searching out a bargain or looking for something they have lost. People generally ignore each other in charity shops, and the one nearest to my house usually has an old woman dozing behind the counter who only wakes properly when you clear your throat standing right in front of her. She takes my money without a word and I leave with my purchase and a quick 'thank you', and then I am out in the open and on my way home. I bring home the teddy bears and clean them carefully, because I hate the idea of germs being on any of my collections. They are arranged on a bookcase, stuffed into the shelves and piled on top. In silence, I take them all off. I usually put them on the bed while I count them, but I'm too agitated to patiently arrange them. I breathe a little easier now that I am in this safe space, inhaling its protected air.

In silence, I pick up the first soft teddy bear, with his lush brown fur, gleaming black eyes, red sewn-on mouth and large round ears. I crush him to me and then I put him back on the bookcase. 'One,' I whisper. Then I lean down and pick up the next one.

As the night grows later, and my certainty over what I have done fades, I listen for the ping sound on my phone that will indicate the arrival of an email. I listen hard as I whisper-count my way through the bears, taking comfort in their softness and in the love that they still hold in their fur.

CHAPTER TWENTY-TWO

LESLIE

9.15 p.m.

The door to the house opens and Leslie feels sick at what she's going to see. Does whoever lives in the run-down house have her child? Who is it? What have they done with her? *Oh Millie, oh sweetheart, I am so sorry I left you. I'm so sorry.*

A light goes on over the front door and everything is illuminated. A man stands at the door, tall, dressed in a pink shirt, and behind him Leslie gets a glimpse of a little girl in pyjamas covered in red love hearts, just like the pyjamas Millie has. Her breath catches in her throat as the policewoman at the door says, 'I'm sorry to bother you, but we've had reports of a missing child possibly being in this house...'

'What?' says the man, who has a thick brown beard, instantly aggressive. The policewoman obviously takes one step back, because the camera moves a little further away.

'Daddy, Daddy,' says the child, reaching her arms up to him to be picked up, and Leslie sees her properly then.

She has long fine black hair just like Millie does, but her

skin is darker and her wide eyes fringed by long lashes are brown in the light from the phone camera.

The man reaches down and lifts her up. She is holding a tiny stuffed rabbit in one hand and she snuggles into him, pushing the rabbit between him and her.

'What are you talking about?' he asks. 'Stella is right here, aren't you, love? What do you mean, a missing child? I've already had a fright today when that old woman peered at me from next door. I thought that house was supposed to be empty, but there she was. Who exactly are you looking for? Stella is right here and her mother knows she's with me. Did she call you? Has my ex-wife called you?' His voice rises a notch, his eyes narrow. Leslie can see that behind his aggression is fear that his daughter will be taken from him, and she assumes that a nasty divorce is the cause of his wariness. But he is not holding Leslie's child.

'No, sir. I apologise, we're looking for Millie Everleigh – she's three years old and she's missing. Have you seen the news?'

'Oh,' says the man, and Leslie watches him hold his daughter just a little tighter, keeping her safe the way Leslie failed to keep Millie safe. 'I did see that, but I've been unpacking so I didn't pay much attention. I've only just moved in. Can you please stop filming my child? That's most inappropriate.'

'You're a policewoman,' says the child, and it's obvious then that she's a couple of years older than Millie. Small with dark hair like Millie, but not Millie at all.

Leslie feels her shoulders sag, the tension in her jaw release, and she hears Constable Willow speaking on the phone. 'Not her,' he says.

'Right,' says Constable Dickerson, clicking off the video. 'I'm sorry about that, but it did sound credible.' He drops his gaze to the carpet and Leslie cannot even be angry with him.

'I understand,' she says sadly. 'I understand.'

Randall has not taken their child to a house next to the golf course. The idea that she would think her husband capable of such a thing is shocking and disturbing. She is not thinking straight right now. Their daughter is still missing and they might never know where she is and what happened to her. Leslie turns away and rests her head against the cold glass of the window, staring at the moon. 'Star light, star bright,' she whispers, and she doesn't register that everyone has left until she turns back.

Randall hasn't stayed, and she doesn't blame him. He knew she thought that he had something to do with Millie going missing, and even though he was not the man in the pink shirt, she's still not completely certain that he isn't involved. Her husband is, supposedly, not who she thinks he is. The little girl in the house was not Millie, Shelby is not telling the truth, and Leslie doesn't know if she will survive this, if she can keep going and survive this.

CHAPTER TWENTY-THREE

SHELBY

She closes the door most of the way, leaving it open enough that Kate can't say she's trying to hide something. As she starts to move away from the door, she hears her mother having a whispered conversation on the phone.

'Just come home already. This is getting ridiculous,' she says, and Shelby knows it's Trevor she's talking to. She doesn't go back to her bed, but stands behind the door, holding her breath.

'What?' says her mum, her voice rising a little before dipping back down. 'I didn't say that. I never told you that. I need you here. Stop trying to always be the good guy. They have enough people and they'll find her, just come home.' She sounds really angry. 'You should have paid more attention. If you want to be the hero, you need to be able to think straight. Just come home and leave them to it. It will sort itself out with or without you.'

Shelby lets her breath out slowly, carefully, not wanting to alert her mother, and then she takes a long breath in and holds it again. Her mother is irritated, angry even. This day is not going how she wants it to go. Selfish, she thinks. That's just selfish.

'No, no,' moans her mother. 'I want some time, just the two of us. Look, leave it now, just come home. Come home right now. I don't want to have to tell you again. They don't care that you're trying to help. The whole world is trying to help and they'll find her. I need you here.'

Bianca is talking to him like he's a child, like he's Shelby's age. But he's not. He's really not, no matter how much he tries to talk to her about Snapchat and Instagram and TikTok. He's not her age.

Her mother ends the call and Shelby darts back to her bed, wrapping her blanket around herself as her mum walks into her room. 'I hoped you would sleep for longer.'

'There's no news, is there?' asks Shelby hopefully.

'No,' says her mother shortly. 'I would tell you, obviously.'

'What were you talking to Trevor about?' asks Shelby, and she is surprised that she feels nervous asking the question.

'Nothing you need to worry about,' says her mother, but she sounds kind of sad. 'Nothing at all.'

CHAPTER TWENTY-FOUR

RUTH

I open my phone and find the news site I follow.

There's an article about the missing little girl, another picture of her at the top. In this one she is obviously at a beach, because behind her I can see the blue line of the sea. She is wearing a large floppy pink sunhat and the picture is a close-up of her face. She's not smiling but concentrating on something, and her blue eyes are wide and beautiful, her lips slightly parted. I wonder what exactly she was looking at or listening to.

There have been unconfirmed reports of Millie Everleigh being found at a house in West Hills. Police have yet to make a statement, but sources have said that police were called to a house where the missing child had been sighted. More news as it comes to hand.

I gasp. Found – they've found her – but then I scroll down a bit more and see that she is still missing, still gone. I knew it couldn't be that easy.

Update: unconfirmed reports about the location of Millie Everleigh have been found to be false. Millie Everleigh is still missing and the public are urged to keep a look out.

I don't read the rest, because the site is only repeating what has already been said.

Why won't she contact me? Why can't this be over? I look at the neatly stacked teddy bears on the large timber bookshelf, then I get up and in silence I throw them all on the floor again. This will never be over. It feels like it will never be over.

CHAPTER TWENTY-FIVE

LESLIE

10.00 p.m.

In her bed, with the duvet tucked around her legs, Leslie feels her head dropping to her chest even though she is sitting up straight. She slips into a dream and hears Millie shouting, 'Mummy, come on, Mummy – I'm ready, come and find me.' Her head jerks up and she looks frantically around her bedroom, but there is only silence to greet her. She had felt her little girl in the room, smelled her tutti-frutti body wash, cloyingly sweet but capable of producing large, round bath bubbles.

But her child is not here and the smell that filled her dream is instantly replaced by the more muted sandalwood fragrance of Randall's aftershave that clings to the air.

She picks up her laptop from her bedside table and opens it, clicking on the file where she has stored endless pictures of her daughter, starting with five minutes after she was born, scrunch-faced with a shock of black hair. She clicks onto a picture of her aged one, a pudgy hand reaching out to grab at the chocolate cake Leslie had made her. She traces her finger over a picture of Millie at two years old, her arms wrapped around a spatula, a bizarre comfort object for a few weeks. She had gone every-where with it, even taking it to bed with her, until one day she lost interest. She clicks over to a picture of Millie at her third birthday party, watching the clown they had hired to entertain her pre-school class. He had brought a giant bubble wand and Millie hadn't even wanted him to stop producing the iridescent bubbles so they could have her pink unicorn birthday cake. Leslie touches her chest, struggling with the feeling of a hand gripping her heart. How can this be it? How can this be the last year she has pictures of her child?

She closes her eyes and breathes in and out. Her work email is filled with messages, but everyone will have to wait – maybe forever. Her desire to be more than Millie's mother, to carve out a space for herself in the professional world, stings her with guilt. How could she have ever wanted more than her little girl? She looks at the window, where the curtains are open and occa-sionally light bounces up from the journalists and television crews who have remained, waiting for news. She's sure the neighbours must be hating this. The families on both sides of them have teenage children who carry phones and are always locatable. She wishes now she had bought Millie one of those watches that allow parents to track their children, but Millie never left the house without her. She was always with an adult or a babysitter. She was always safe. Except she had not been safe today.

Time is inching towards midnight, towards another day, and soon Millie will have been missing for the full twenty-four hours. Each time she looks at her phone or a clock and more time has passed, Leslie feels her panic and anxiety rising to fever pitch. If a child is not located in the first twenty-four hours, are they ever located? Does it mean they're... She doesn't want to think the word, can't bear to think the word.

She changes screens on her laptop, types in 'How many children under the age of five go missing in Australia?' But the results are of no use. Children are taken by their parents in the case of divorce or separation, but that's not really like what has happened to Millie. Historical cases of missing children make her shiver in the warm room. A young child going missing, a child who is never found, becomes part of history. A cautionary tale for all parents. She cannot imagine how mothers go on after that.

Without meaning to, she clicks onto her work emails and is just about to close the screen when she sees the subject heading on the top email: *This is about your child*. Her heart thuds in her chest. Another troll? Probably, and possibly even spam containing a virus. There is no low people won't sink to, but she has to know what it says. She takes a breath, her fingers shaking slightly, and then she opens the email.

It's from an address she doesn't recognise. *Take a look at this*, reads the message, and there is a link, which she clicks on, knowing that she shouldn't because it might damage her computer or lead her to some hideous, gruesome site, but powerless to stop herself. She shoves the blanket off her legs, sweat beading on her face. It's a newspaper article from what looks like a local paper called *The Alex Heights Gazette* in Perth. Leslie has never heard of the suburb, but she's never been to Perth either.

The article is short and is headed: *Local teacher moving on*. The print is small and slightly hard to read, but she peers at the date. Friday 18 November 2005. Where was she all those years ago? She was in her early twenties then, filled with hope for the future, just starting out in advertising after finishing her degree in graphic design. *Tony Richardson (31) has left Alex Heights High School after three years teaching computer science to students. Mr Richardson was a popular teacher who also ran the local community drama club. Last year they performed a spirited production of* A Midsummer Night's Dream. *Principal of Alex*

Heights, Mr Carl Donnelly, said, 'It is always sad to see a teacher leave, but sometimes people need to move on.'

Leslie snorts at the ridiculous article, accompanied by a grainy picture of a man with his arms raised obviously mid-sentence as he gestures towards someone else. It must be a picture of the teacher directing the play or something like that. Why would someone send her this rubbish? She moves her hand to delete the article before it infects her computer with some kind of virus, although she might be too late already.

And then she looks at the photo that accompanies the article again. The man is familiar, though the picture is not very good quality. As she stares at the image, she feels suddenly queasy as she starts to recognise the face. It was a long time ago, but there is more than a passing resemblance. Slightly out of focus, but obviously him the more she looks at it. She raises her hand to her mouth. It's him, but that's not his name. The more she stares, the more certain she becomes. Why has he changed his name?

This has something to do with Millie, she knows it does. She needs to find Constable Dickerson and show him, tell him, say that it's all connected. She stands up, adrenaline running through her so she is wide awake, and as she does so, the bedroom door opens and Randall walks in.

'Les, are you okay?' he asks. 'You've gone really pale.'

CHAPTER TWENTY-SIX

SHELBY

It's late, and she can hear the soft murmurs from the television in the living room. Kate, the young constable, has left, telling them that someone will be over in the morning. They have obviously decided that Shelby is not going to remember anything between now and then.

Her mother is waiting for Trevor to come home, but he's insisting on helping with the search, which Shelby knows is making her mother angry. She is scrolling through her phone, scared to get another message and yet waiting for it. Maybe if she replies and says she's going to tell, this will all be over. Maybe her whole world will blow up, but at least it will be over. People are posting messages on her Instagram filled with love hearts, telling her they are thinking of her and that they are here if she needs to talk. She's famous, hideously, heartbreakingly famous. Nothing like this has ever happened to any one of her friends.

Kiera's texts have kept coming, some whiny, some mean.

I'm sorry it happened.

Shelby hadn't believed that one.

Please don't tell anyone about me being there. I hope we're still best friends after this.

The last text should make her feel scared, but it just makes her really, really sad.

This was your fault, Shelby. If you don't reply, I'm going to tell my mum. What is wrong with you? I hate you!

Kiera is not who she thought she was. It seems no one is. Everyone is hiding their true selves. Those selves only come out when things go wrong, and Shelby wonders who *she* is, who she truly is. Is she a good person who will tell everyone what happened, or is she a terrible person who will tell everyone what happened? Which one is the right Shelby to be if both are actually the same?

Kiera is afraid of what's going to happen when everyone knows she was there – and what happened because she was there.

In her head, Shelby is going over it, what she has kept from everyone, and trying to find a way to explain it without anyone else getting hurt. She puts her phone down and stares up at the ceiling, tracing some delicate cracks in the white paint with her eyes.

The terrifying fear as Millie ran and she and Kiera ran after her returns. She was so quick. She just shot right out of the front door, across the yard and out of the open gate. Shelby had buzzed Kiera in when she arrived and Kiera had obviously not closed the gate after she came into the front garden. If Kiera had closed the gate, if she had just closed the gate... but she hadn't. It happened so fast and yet Shelby's legs felt heavy, like she couldn't move quickly enough, like she was going slowly as she ran after her little sister, who darted into the road, just darted sideways and out onto the road, where a car was coming for her, straight for her. 'Millie, no!' Shelby thinks she shouted – thinks, but maybe it was only in her head.

And then the car was there, right in the middle of the road, heading for Millie, who was too small to be seen by the person driving. It was heading right for her. In her bedroom now, Shelby moans softly at the anguish that coursed through her as she realised that she wouldn't get to her sister quickly enough and she grasped what was about to happen.

But it didn't happen. It didn't.

Millie could have been hit by the car – could have been tossed in the air and killed because she was so small – but the car stopped, brakes screeching, tyres burning, the rubber smell filling the air on the quiet street.

It stopped.

CHAPTER TWENTY-SEVEN

RUTH

I complete my teddy bear count, relishing the way each of them feels in my hands. It's late, nearly eleven, later than I've been awake in years. But I can't go to sleep. I have to see this through. I look at my childhood bed. The place where I lay and dreamed, where I worried and cried, where I thought about what life would have been like for me if not for a certain teacher. Some girls, some women get away only slightly scathed by something like what happened to me. They are hurt, damaged but able to move forward. Perhaps if I'd had therapy that worked, if I'd had someone to speak to that I trusted, even just someone who believed in me – but I didn't. He was so good at what he did.

'What is wrong with you?' my mother yelled when I refused to attend school any more.

'Why are you like this?' she begged when I locked myself in my room and refused to come and eat dinner.

'What is going to happen to you?' she asked me just before she died, the cigarettes having done what every doctor promises they will do. Her damaged lungs could not get enough air. It is a horribly cruel way to die, and at the end, all I could do was manage her pain. She liked me to sing to her, hymns, mostly, like 'Amazing Grace'. She enjoyed listening to me talk about some of her more outlandish behaviour. 'Remember when you pulled me out of school when I was ten and we drove straight to the airport to go to Queensland?'

'All you did was fuss and complain that you hadn't had time to plan and pack.' She nodded her head, the memory making her smile.

'Remember when we ate cake for breakfast for a whole week, a different one every day?'

She had chuckled at that, and then wheezed and coughed. 'You told me it would rot your teeth.'

I was always a child who liked routine and planning. There were rules to living your life and my mother never seemed interested in any of them. I never had a bedtime and she didn't care if my homework got done or not. But she loved me, I know she did. She just didn't believe me when she should have done. That was her greatest failing.

I also don't know what's going to happen to me in the future, but it feels like this is the start of something. Once he is exposed, once all is revealed, I can move on. Maybe, perhaps, possibly, I can move on. I look at the bed again. That's probably not going to happen. But at least I will have told the truth, exposed him to the world, made everyone see he can't be believed. At least I will have done that, and whatever happens then, it will still be better than where I am now. Once he has paid for what he did, my mind can release him. That's all I really want – for my mind to be free of him.

CHAPTER TWENTY-EIGHT

LESLIE

10.45 p.m.

Leslie turns the computer around to face her husband. 'Can you explain this?' she asks.

He peers at the screen, then he takes off his glasses, polishes them on his shirt, not meeting her gaze. He places them on his face again and looks at her. 'Who is that?' he asks.

'You tell me,' she says.

He looks at the picture again. 'Oh, right... oh yes, I see it now. What does that have to do with anything?'

'I need to talk to Shelby,' says Leslie. 'I need to tell the police and go and talk to Shelby. I'm going to call the constable.' She stands up, picking up her laptop, energised now that she has something, something that may help, that may be a clue as to where Millie is. She doesn't know how, but somebody else out there seems to know something more, and they want her to understand that Millie disappearing is something more than just a child who ran away.

'Wait... wait, please,' says Randall. 'Just give me a minute, just a minute.' He paces back and forth a little and she sees his lips move as he thinks through what to do. She is instantly irritated.

'Where is my daughter, Randall?' she hisses. '*She* doesn't have a minute. She's missing, gone. Where is she? Are you telling me this isn't something I should tell the police? Shelby has been strange for the last few months, behaving badly... just... It's all you and Bianca have talked about, and Bianca thinks it's because she spends time here, but maybe it's not that.'

'Les, just... let me think.' He pushes his hands through his hair. 'Let's go and talk to Shelby first. If we tell the police and then she gets scared and clams up... I mean, if he has something to do with any of this, she's scared for a reason, she's... This is making me feel sick. Shelby and Millie were here, at home together in our house. What could he possibly have to do with anything?'

'I want to tell the police. They need to trace the email, find this person – ask him or her what they know.'

'No,' he says, almost shouts, 'no... Shelby first. I'm begging you. I think... I think she can explain, and then...'

'Then what?'

'I don't know,' he says, shaking his head. 'I don't know.'

'They won't let us leave, you know that, and Shelby is probably asleep. We need to put this in the hands of the police.' She gets up and goes to her closet, pulling on a heavy jumper because she's cold, her body shivering as she tries in vain to piece everything together.

'I'll tell them we need a walk, just a walk in the fresh air. Let's get to Shelby and then we'll know if it's a coincidence, because maybe it is and it has nothing to do with anything.'

Leslie nods, because there is no point in arguing with him. He's still protecting his daughter.

Ten minutes later, they are downstairs, bundled up in coats.

'We want to go out for a bit,' says Randall. 'To get some air.'

'It's late for a walk,' says Constable Dickerson. 'We need you here.' He looks tired, and she can see that he is eating chocolate to keep himself awake. The kitchen smells of constantly brewed coffee and the melting sweetness of the caramel chocolate he has opened next to him.

'My wife...' begins Randall. 'Leslie is not coping right now. Just some air, just around the block. We have our phones. We will be minutes away.' He is convincing, sincere, not a man you should doubt or question. But she has been questioning him, all day she has been questioning him.

The constable holds up his hand. 'Five minutes,' he tells them. 'Go out the back, because there are still some journalists standing in the front. They're a persistent bunch, I'll give them that.'

Outside, they walk quickly and Leslie is surprised at how soon they are shrouded in silent darkness after the lights and noise of her house.

Your husband is not who he says he is. The words come back to haunt her. Why would she have received that message? As a car pulls into view, Randall lifts his hand. He has already called the Uber and directed it to meet them two streets away from their home.

Why would she have been sent that message? It's not her husband in the photo. It's not. Why would someone think it was? She thinks back over the day. There have been cameras everywhere, filming. Perhaps someone saw him standing next to her? Perhaps someone...

'He hugged me,' she says as they climb into the Uber.

'What?' says Randall, and he leans forward and checks that the man knows where to go. The driver is large and silent, only nodding. Leslie wonders how often he is called to the suburbs close to midnight. Wonders if he has been following the news, if he has any inkling who they are.

'He hugged me,' she says again. 'So many people have

hugged me today and he was definitely one of them. He came up to me just after the press conference and hugged me. Maybe they were still filming; maybe the person who sent the text and the article saw that and made a mistake.'

'What does it mean, Les? So he changed his name – so what?'

'I don't know,' she says. 'But it means something, it has to, and it has to have something to do with what happened today. It just has to.'

The car pulls away, cocooning them inside, keeping out the cold and the sounds of the wheels on the road, and she watches the houses they pass, where only a few lights are still on. It's time for sleep. It's the very end of the day and she should be fast asleep with her daughter in the next room. She should be but she's not, and that's not her fault. She is certain of that now. It's not her fault, but it's someone's fault. It is definitely someone's fault.

CHAPTER TWENTY-NINE

SHELBY

Shelby turns over in bed as the afternoon comes rushing at her as fast as the car rushed at Millie. She remembers her sickening fear. But the car stopped. It didn't hit Millie, it stopped.

Her stomach lurched, relief making her sick.

Millie was frozen right by the bumper, her blue eyes wide in her face, but Shelby knew that she couldn't have understood how close she had come to dying. Leslie always lectured her about staying away from roads, crossing only with an adult or with Shelby and always holding hands. But she didn't understand yet, not yet.

On the pavement, Kiera and Shelby were motionless. They both watched as the door of the car opened and he got out. Shelby knew it was him, had recognised his car right away. She hadn't understood how he was there, because he was supposed to be off doing something else, but she hadn't thought about that then.

'What the hell is going on here?' he said, fury in his voice.

'I have to go,' said Kiera, and she waved and started walking.

'Hey, wait,' he said, and Kiera started running, leaving

Shelby to deal with the mess she had made. Shelby darted into the street and picked up Millie.

'She ran away,' she said. 'She ran away and I couldn't catch her.' Inside her the fear was replaced by a bubble of happiness as her little sister's arms went around her neck. She wanted to shout, to giggle, to jump because Millie was safe. The car had not hit her. Shelby was in trouble, she knew she was in trouble, but Millie was safe and that was all that mattered.

'She could have been killed,' he yelled. 'You're supposed to be taking care of her.'

'I know,' Shelby had yelled back. Millie wrapped her arms tighter around her neck, her body quaking with shock or sadness at Kiera shouting at her, or both. Shelby ran along the pavement, desperate to get back inside the house. 'Sorry, Millie, sorry, Millie, sorry, Millie,' she said as her little sister's arms held on and her body bounced as she ran. She needed her inside and safe, away from the road and all its terrible dangers, away from everything there that could hurt her.

In the house, the warmth from the heater making her sweat, she allowed herself to breathe properly. She put Millie down.

'Why did he shout?' asked Millie.

'Just go sit down,' Shelby said firmly. She turned around to close the door, to lock him out, but he was already there. 'I'm sorry...' she started to say.

'This is completely unacceptable. She's just three years old. Why was that Kiera over here? Did you ask Leslie if you could have a friend over?' His brow was creased, his blue eyes dark and angry.

Her body trembling as the adrenaline left her now that Millie was safe, Shelby couldn't stop a few tears escaping. But she was mostly relieved that nothing had happened to her sister.

'All right,' he said. 'Okay, don't worry. She's fine. Sit down now and I'll get you both something to drink.'

'No, I'll be okay. Leslie will be home soon. Why are you here?'

Millie sat at her little table, picking up a large black crayon. 'I don't like Kiera, she's mean,' she said, drawing a circle and colouring it in in thick black strokes. She didn't know how close her life had been to ending. Just like that, in a split second, she could have been dead, but Shelby didn't have the energy to explain it to her, to make her understand.

'It's a good thing I'm here after what I just saw. Imagine how incredibly upset Leslie would be. I mean, how irresponsible of you, Shelby. I may stay for a bit just so I know everyone is safe. You had no right to have a friend over and I have no idea what could have been going on to make Millie run away. This is all not good.' She hated it when he went into lecture mode, when he tried to tell her what she was doing wrong. The more he told her, the worse she felt and the more she questioned herself. She just wanted him gone.

'No, it's fine,' she said again. She wanted him to go, just go, and then she would sit down at Millie's little table and colour with her. She would tell Millie that Kiera coming over was a secret between the two of them and that she would never let Kiera come over again. She would promise that if Millie kept the secret and didn't tell Leslie about the car and the road, then Shelby would stop being friends with Kiera. She hadn't realised right then that it would not be necessary to tell Millie to keep quiet.

'Sit down,' he said. 'We need to discuss this. I really don't want to have to tell Leslie and your father what I just saw.' An edge to his voice, a slight threat. 'I'll get the juice.'

'Kiera was mean to me,' said Millie, the crayon moving over the page, filling up all the white spaces with black. Shelby knew that she was in trouble. Not just for letting Millie run away, not just for nearly letting her get hit by a car. She was in trouble because he was here. She had wondered why he was there, and how he had known she was alone. She had wondered at the terrible coincidence of him driving up to the house just as Millie ran out into the road. And then she had realised how he had known, realised who had told him, and some stuff came up in her throat but she swallowed to keep it down. She was in trouble and there was nothing she could do about it because she needed to protect Millie.

Shelby willed Leslie to come home. She looked longingly at the door to the kitchen, where she hoped to hear her coming in from the garage, prayed to hear her call, 'Come and help with parcels if you want a treat.' Leslie would see him in the kitchen and everything would be simple and friendly. But Leslie had been gone longer than the hour she said she would be gone. Shelby had looked down at her phone and seen that it was after 1 p.m. She thought about sending her mother a text, but then he walked back into the room with two glasses of juice. 'I don't like apple juice,' she wanted to say, but didn't. No one knew anything about her any more, no one cared what she did and didn't like.

'Here you go,' he said to Millie, placing the juice on her little table.

'Thank you, thank you, thank you,' Millie sang.

'You're a good girl,' he said to her, and he stroked her head, causing her to beam at him. He handed Shelby her glass and said, 'Drink up, there's a good girl.'

Shelby squeezed the glass in her hand, wondering if she could shatter it so apple juice sprayed everywhere and she was forced to run for a rag. Millie was too little to know who he truly was, but then she was surrounded by adults who had no idea who he was either.

'Sit down,' he said again, and finally she sat, placing the untouched glass of juice on the small table at the side of the sofa, pushing it far away from her. She didn't know what else to do. He sat down next to her. She wanted to run, to just get up and run, but she had Millie to watch over. She wondered if she could pick up her sister and then run upstairs and lock them both in Leslie and her father's room. Could she run fast enough?

She knew that if Leslie walked in right now, she would just say, 'Oh, hello, what are you doing here?' and he would answer something like 'Just checking up on Shelby,' and she would believe him – because everyone did.

'I need to go to the bathroom,' she said, starting to stand up, but he grabbed her arm and pulled her back down onto the sofa next to him.

'Sit down,' he said. 'Millie is happy drawing, aren't you, Millie? Shelby and I are going to have a little chat.'

'Chat, chat, chat,' sang Millie, and then she glanced up and looked at Shelby before returning to her drawing, selecting a new piece of paper and a bright purple crayon. Her anger at Kiera forgotten, her dash into the road a memory, her unhappiness gone.

And then…

Shelby closes her eyes, hating that the image is right there, the image of what happened is right there still and she knows it will never go away.

Her door swings open and her mother is standing there. 'Your father and his wife would like to speak to you,' she says, startling Shelby, who hurriedly buries her phone underneath her pillow, her hands trembling. She hadn't heard anyone arrive but she can tell that a whole conversation went on outside her room with her mum trying to stop her dad and Leslie coming in to speak to her and the two of them insisting. All three adults are a little red in the face and Shelby knows that the argument between them would have taken place in harsh whispers. When she was five, she always got more rather than less anxious when her parents lowered their voices. It meant that whatever fight they were having, it was a bad one. The night before they told her they were getting a divorce, the house was almost silent, but if she listened hard enough, she could hear the angry hiss of their fight.

Leslie and her dad crowd into her room and she watches as Leslie glances around, feeling a little ashamed of the mess. Leslie likes things neat, and Shelby tries to keep things tidy at her house, but then there is so much storage – little cupboards and drawers that have been built into her room – that she kind of enjoys organising things there. But here is where she lives, and here is where her life is messy and complicated. So messy, so very complicated.

'You don't have to talk to them if you don't want to,' her mother says, and Shelby feels like the room is too crowded, too stuffy. Her mother wants her to refuse. She knows that. Her heart is racing and she tries to take a deep breath. On any other Saturday night, she would be asleep by now. Everyone in the house would be asleep.

'We really need to speak to you, Shelby,' says her father, and his voice sounds desperate and kind of like he's begging her to talk to them. Both Leslie and her dad look like they're older than they were this morning, when there were wonky pancakes for breakfast and her dad dressed up for his silly golf day, laughing as he made a mess of breakfast so Leslie could have a sleep in.

'I don't mind,' she says. She catches her mum's angry shake of her head. 'It's okay,' she repeats, just to make sure her mother knows it's her decision.

'Fine,' sighs her mother, and she picks up a pile of clean laundry from the rocking chair that has been in Shelby's room since she was a baby and puts it on the floor, sitting down and turning to look at Leslie and Shelby's father.

'Actually, we would prefer...' Leslie starts to say, and then she seems to lose her nerve and she looks at Shelby's dad.

'Can you just give us some time alone with her, please,

Bianca?' her dad says, and Shelby wants to cry for him because he looks so sad and it's all her fault and she can't find a way to fix anything.

'Absolutely not. I will be here when you speak to her, thank you,' says her mother, spitting the words out. Her mother is worried about her and Shelby knows that, but she hates the way she talks to her father and she hates the way she looks at Leslie sometimes, as though she were some dirt on her shoe. She wouldn't say that she loves Leslie, not at all, but sometimes she's... easier to talk to than her own mother.

Her mum is looking at her, eyes narrowed, and Shelby suddenly knows, the way you sometimes just know something, that it's not that she's worried about her. She's worried about what she is going to say. She gets a strange feeling inside her body and she rubs at her face, hot and itchy. She feels like a girl in a horror movie who has just realised she has nowhere else to run.

Her mother told him she was babysitting; told him she was alone with Millie. *Who are you?* Shelby wants to say to her. *You don't seem like my mum, so who are you? Who have you become? Which of your true selves am I seeing right now?* Her mother wants her to keep quiet, not because she's worried about Shelby, but because she's worried about someone else.

She sits up higher on her bed and tries to take a deep breath, but it gets caught and she coughs. In her head there is a humming noise, and she meets her mother's gaze, a horrible thought lodging in her brain.

Her mother knows exactly what happened.

But can she know? How can she know and not have said anything?

Her mother shakes her head at her again, confirming that she needs Shelby to keep quiet.

As she tries to take in the terrible idea that her mother knows – that she has known all along as the whole suburb searches for Millie – she feels a wave of sadness crest inside her. Her mother knows and yet she has chosen to remain silent, to protect the person she loves the most.

And even worse than that, it's possible that her mother has kind of understood what Shelby has been trying to say but not say for a few months already.

And now Shelby is afraid.

Does her mother know where Millie is, where Millie's body is? And what will she do if Shelby tells the truth? She cannot say anything. She will have to lie if her mother is sitting there looking at her. She cannot say the words if her mother's fierce gaze is on her.

'Bianca,' says her father, standing up straighter, 'Leslie and I are going to speak to Shelby alone. That's what going to happen now. I don't have the patience for any of your crap. Leave the room and leave us alone.'

Shelby feels her mouth drop open a little. Her father never, never speaks to anyone like that, and when she looks at Leslie and her mum, she can see the same shock on their faces. Her mother gives herself a little shake, ridding herself of her surprise.

'Shelby wants me to stay, don't you, Shelby?' she says.

Even though she knows it's cold outside, Shelby gets off the bed and pushes at her bedroom window, opening it slightly so that cold air blows in. The adults in the room are all silent as they wait for her to answer, and she wishes that it was two days ago, before all this happened. She wishes she had talked to her father, told him the truth about what she's dealing with, wishes she was anywhere else but here, was anyone else but Shelby.

But she is here now, and nothing will change unless she tells the truth. She cannot remain in this horrible limbo and she cannot keep the truth from Leslie and her father any longer.

She sits back down on the bed. 'I don't want you to stay,' she whispers, her eyes focused on the furry blue blanket on her bed so she will not have to look at her mother.

Her mother doesn't say anything else. She just gets up and leaves the room, slamming the door behind her the way Shelby is never allowed to slam the door.

'Listen, Shelby,' says her father when it's obvious her mother has walked away, although Shelby wouldn't put it past her to have her ear pressed up against the door, 'we need to ask you something about this afternoon.'

'Okay,' says Shelby, wary, tired, sad.

'It's about Trevor,' says Leslie.

'Trevor,' repeats Shelby, her voice flat.

'Yes,' replies her father.

Shelby nods slowly, a tear inching its way down her cheek.

'Oh sweetheart,' says Leslie, sitting down on the bed. 'What happened? What happened?'

CHAPTER THIRTY

RUTH

I cannot stay awake any more. In my old bedroom, I curl up on
the floor with a blanket from the sofa. I curl up small and I wait
with my phone clutched in my hand. I have failed at what I set
out to do. She will not read the email and expose him to the
world for me. I will have to go over there in the morning. I will
have to go to the child's house and tell everyone there the truth.
I look at the bed again, and then I curl myself into a ball on the
floor and I sleep.

CHAPTER THIRTY-ONE

LESLIE

11.00 p.m.

Leslie feels frustration building up inside her as she watches her stepdaughter hunched over on the bed, tears running down her cheeks. If they yell, if they push, they won't get the answers they need, but she can feel that something terrible has happened, and what she's worried about is Trevor turning up before Shelby has said anything.

He's not here, which means he could be searching for Millie, or he could be on his way home, and she has no idea what he might have had to do with her baby girl going missing. What does he know? What does Shelby know?

She thinks about the article she read about Trevor, who used to be someone else entirely. Why would a teacher have left his school and moved states and changed his name? What was he running away from? And then the thought she's been trying not to acknowledge strikes her like a blow to the head.

'Shelby,' she says softly, 'did Trevor…' She twists her fingers together as she tries to think of a way to say what she wants to say, a way to say something she's never thought she would have to say, to ask a question she never thought she would have to ask. And while she is thinking, she looks at her stepdaughter and sees something in the girl's face. Shelby wants to speak. She wants to tell them the truth, but she needs help, because she is still just a child.

She stops her fingers moving and clasps her hands in front of her to prevent any hair-pulling, and then she clears her throat and says softly, 'Did Trevor do something to you that you didn't like? Did he do something to you or to...' and here she pauses as she swallows, acid rising in her throat, 'Millie?'

Behind her, Randall is standing with his hands in his pockets, and as she says the words, she can feel his body getting hotter, as though anger is literally setting him on fire, but he keeps quiet, because even though he doesn't want to hear that something has happened to his daughter, to his daughters, they need to know.

'He...' says Shelby, 'he... he says he's not doing anything, just being friendly, and... trying to make us into a proper family so Mum can be happy. He says... I'm imagining things and being difficult.'

'What?' asks Randall. 'What does that mean?'

The door bursts open and Bianca comes into the room. She has obviously been listening at the door.

'What on earth is going on in here?' she yells. 'What are you trying to get her to say?'

'Please, Bianca,' appeals Leslie, 'please just let her speak.'

'No,' shouts Bianca. 'I want you two out of my house right now. Just get out. It's not my daughter's fault that your child is missing, that you left Shelby alone all afternoon with an undisciplined toddler who has now run away, and I can't believe that you would somehow try to turn this on Trevor for some ungodly reason. What on earth would he have to do with any of this? Are you both mad? You sound completely mad and you're pressuring her to say things, actually trying to put words into her mouth. It's disgusting, *you're* disgusting.' Her face is bright red and Leslie can see that she is sweating slightly, despite the cold air blowing in from the window Shelby opened. The calm control she has over everything in her life seems to have disappeared.

And Leslie knows it's because she's worried that what she's heard Shelby say is the truth. Leslie would believe her child first and then her husband, but Bianca has made up her own mind without even really listening.

'Just get out, both of you, right now, before I call the police,' Bianca shouts.

'Hey, Bianca, I'm home,' they hear as the front door opens. On the bed, Shelby freezes, her eyes the only thing moving as they swing wildly between her mother and father. 'Where is everyone?'

Leslie can feel the child's fear running through her own body. Shelby is afraid of Trevor. She is afraid, and because she has been silenced, they will never know what he's done.

'Shelby, please,' she whispers.

'He touches me,' says Shelby, her voice rough, as though it hasn't been used. 'He says he's my friend but that's not how friends touch each other. He does it and says it never happened or I'm making it up. But I know what he's doing, and yesterday—'

'Yesterday what?' says Trevor. He has stepped into the room, a sickly smile on his face.

Randall turns to face him and Leslie can see that he's going to hit him.

'Not telling lies again, is she?' asks Trevor, and he shakes his head sadly, even as he steps behind Bianca so that Randall will have to go through his ex-wife to get to him. He is a conventionally good-looking man, but there is something bland and plain about his face. He could be anyone and no one. But he's not anyone, Leslie knows now – he's a stepfather to a young child and he's been assaulting her. Shelby is not lying, not exaggerating. Leslie can feel the anguished truth in the girl's words, and she wants to spit in Trevor's face.

'I really don't want to have to tell your father and Leslie what you did, Shelby. Now just tell them that you're making stuff up, that you're lying. You have to understand, Randall, that Shelby didn't want her mother to get married again. It's been hard enough for her to have a stepmother; of course she didn't want a stepfather as well. But that's no reason to tell terrible lies, is it, Shelby? No reason to make your mother unhappy by telling lies.' To go with the bland, smooth face is a smooth, bland voice that seems to hold no threat at all, and yet Leslie can hear it's there.

'It's not a lie,' whispers Shelby.

Randall steps towards Bianca. 'I will kill you,' he growls.

Trevor steps back and holds up his hands, a slight tinge of panic in his voice now. 'You know what happens to liars, don't you, Shelby? Now tell the truth. Tell them what you did to Millie, or *I* will tell them and then you'll go to prison. You will go to prison for a very long time.'

Shelby bursts into noisy sobs.

'Leave – both of you,' screams Bianca. She turns to Trevor. 'I told you to come home. I told you to come and deal with things here. Why didn't you listen to me?' she yells.

'Shut it, Bianca. Now both of you get out of my house with your filthy accusations,' says Trevor, arms waving, fists clenched.

Leslie wants to grab her stepchild and shake her until her teeth rattle and the answers fall out. But she also wants to grab her and run, away from this house where she is being damaged and no one seems to care.

She swings round and faces Bianca and Trevor. 'I'm calling the police. They can deal with this.'

As she takes her phone out of her pocket, Trevor lunges for

her, Randall goes for him and Bianca screams. Trevor gets to her first and shoves her hard, pushing her backwards. She falls, and her head connects with the corner of Shelby's bedside table. She feels a sharp, intense pain and slumps to the floor, dizzy, with ringing ears.

Through the high-pitched screaming in her head, she hears the sound of skin on skin and she knows that Randall has punched Trevor.

'Trevor – wait,' Bianca calls, and then everything goes black.

CHAPTER THIRTY-TWO

SHELBY

Shelby pushes herself back further on her bed. She can't believe that just happened, that she is sitting here in the middle of this nightmare. This is not how grown-ups behave. What is wrong with all of them?

Leslie is crumpled on the floor, lying on her side, and Shelby can see a trickle of blood running down the back of her neck. Her father looks around the room frantically and then crouches down by his wife.

'Les, Les, are you okay?' he says, as he touches her shoulder. He pulls her body to lie her flat on the ground. 'I think we need an ambulance,' he says, and looks at the door. Her mother and Trevor have disappeared. Trevor ran and her mother followed him.

'She's gone after him,' says Shelby bitterly. 'She always chooses him.' Somewhere inside her, she knows that one day she will look back at this time and realise that this was the moment she understood her mother didn't love her the way she should, the way Leslie loves Millie, the way she assumed every mother loves their child. And this will always cause her pain.

But right now, she's overwhelmed and fearful, exhausted and sad. She cannot think straight.

All the things she has wanted to tell her father pile up inside her, everything she has been keeping secret because she thought she was wrong at first and then she thought it was a misunderstanding and then he told her she was imagining it. She has been questioning herself for months, wondering if she is stupid or a bad person, and every time she has said something even slightly negative about him to her mother, she has been told, 'Don't you think I deserve to be happy like your father is?' She has never told her mother the whole truth. Instead, she has said things that are of no consequence, testing the waters to see if her mother will listen and believe her.

'Trevor seems to get angry with me a lot,' she had said after he had yelled at her for talking during the news on television.

'You need to learn to respect his time. If he's in front of the television, just be quiet,' her mother had replied.

'Trevor always bangs on the bathroom door when I'm taking a shower. Can you ask him to stop?'

'It's not his fault we can't afford a two-bathroom house. We both work as hard as we can. I don't have the luxury of being married to a man as rich as your father. Respect the fact that Trevor needs to get to work or wherever he's going. You're a child, Shelby, know your place.'

'I don't like that Trevor hugs me so much.'

'He's trying to be kind, to be a part of this family. I'm sure you don't mind hugging Leslie. Stop making everything about you. Be kind to him. I don't want to end up alone because you're having issues that have nothing to do with Trevor.'

Shelby has understood from everything her mother said, from every reaction she's had, that she will not be believed, because even she herself has questioned what's happening.

Nothing he does is big enough for her to point to and say 'he did this'. Instead, everything is just something small, something she could ignore if she wanted to, something she should probably simply dismiss; but she can't do that, and it's exhausting. She feels hunted in her own home. She makes sure to shower when he's out and get changed with her rocking chair against the door, because he doesn't believe bedroom doors should be locked in case of a fire. A few months ago, when the summer heat was still hanging around, she had gone to sleep in shorty pyjamas and woken up in the middle of the night with her duvet on the floor and him in her bedroom. 'It's cold,' he told her when she startled and moved away from him. 'I was worried you'd freeze in those little pyjamas.' Trying to convince herself that he was being kind, that he was only showing concern, was becoming more and more impossible. It was gross and made her feel disgusting.

It feels like he's put some sort of spell on her mother and she can't see what's right in front of her. But maybe Shelby is making a big deal out of nothing, just being overly sensitive, making it all about her.

Every time she has gone to stay with her father and Leslie, she has thought about telling them what is going on, but Trevor always makes her feel like nothing is really happening.

'I don't like it when you hug me for so long,' she told him, thinking that maybe she just needed to express herself.

'What kind of a girl doesn't like a hug? Your mother keeps telling me to try and get along with you, and I am trying, but you're making it so hard. Why do you want us all to be unhappy, Shelby? What's wrong with you?'

'Stop coming into my room without knocking,' she told him.

'I was looking for a charger. It's not my fault you take the only one in the house that works. What are you accusing me of?'

And that's the problem. She doesn't know. She can't explain it properly. When she reads about this kind of stuff on the internet, it's big and ugly, with girls really getting hurt, but he isn't doing anything that she could say is wrong. It's little things, things that make her uncomfortable, and she keeps trying to convince herself it's just because she isn't used to being in the house with him.

But this afternoon, everything changed. This afternoon, he finally did something and the person who saw, the precious little person who was too young to even know what she was looking at, leapt in to defend her.

'Call an ambulance,' her father barks at her now, making her jump, and she grabs her phone and dials ooo, but even before she presses the call button, Leslie opens her eyes and says, 'No, no ambulance. I'm fine.'

Shelby can see that she is definitely not fine. Her face is sheet white and her lips are tinged with blue. But she puts her phone down anyway.

Leslie tries to sit up. 'Tell us what happened, Shelby,' she says. 'Where is Millie?'

CHAPTER THIRTY-THREE

RUTH

I wake an hour later and pick up my phone, glancing anxiously at the screen for some kind of reply from her, some kind of acknowledgement – but there's nothing. It's midnight, but I know there's no way I'm going to get back to sleep.

I glance at my childhood bed, covered with the blanket my grandmother knitted. It's made from different-coloured squares, but she didn't just choose a few colours, she chose many colours. I have been looking at the blanket for years, and, even now, sometimes I spot a colour somewhere between blue and green, or somewhere between red and pink, and realise that I have never seen it before. I love that blanket. It made me feel safe when little else could. But I don't need it as much anymore. Not now that I have my piles.

I leave the room and use the bathroom, and then I open my computer and watch a news clip of the first press conferences about the missing little girl, making sure to force myself to watch to the end. I don't look away and I don't turn it off. I am searching for something, though I'm not sure what. Maybe some clue as to why the mother wouldn't have contacted me. Did she not want to know the truth? I told her the article was to do with her child. She should have contacted me by now – unless she didn't care, and I know that's a possibility. My mother didn't care. My mother was taken in by him, charmed and gaslighted. She told me I was the one making a mistake, that I was the one in the wrong. She wasn't the first woman that happened to, I'm sure. When I was thirteen, he was twenty-four. My mother was too old for him, but it was never her he was interested in. He's much older now and his new wife looks to be younger than forty, but she doesn't know he's not interested in her. Instead, he is focused on the little girl with fine black hair like her mother. He'll wait for her to get a little older, and then...

I watch the first press conference, from the moment the police constable raises his hands and says, 'Thanks, everyone.' I watch it once and then I watch it again, horror creeping through my veins, because I am not seeing what I thought I would see. I should have seen this the first time. I should have watched it properly, because I am not seeing what I should be seeing.

The man standing next to the mother – the man who I can see now is the father of the missing little girl – is not Touchy Tony. It's not him.

CHAPTER THIRTY-FOUR

LESLIE

12.00 a.m.

Leslie lets Randall help her up into a sitting position on the floor next to Shelby's bed. She tries to look for Bianca and Trevor, but they are gone. Each object she focuses on shimmers and waves. It's easier if she closes her eyes. She does need to go to the hospital, she knows that. She can feel the warm blood on the back of her neck, and she raises a hand to touch where she has hit her head, feeling the wet matted hair there.

'We need to get you to a doctor,' says Randall firmly.

'We will, but let her speak, please, Randall. Just let her tell us where Millie is.' Her voice is weak, her breathing difficult and her body feels strange, but she needs to know.

'I don't know,' says Shelby, her voice catching in her throat. 'I don't know where he took her.'

'He's gone,' says Bianca.

She is back in the room, Leslie realises, her voice coming from the doorway. Leslie turns her head to look at her, slumped against the door frame. Bianca looks old, haggard. Her hair is a mess and black streaks from her mascara stain her cheeks. She has been crying, but Leslie knows she has only been crying for herself. She is the most selfish woman Leslie has ever known, and she feels a terrible sadness for Shelby that she's had to live with her as a mother. Mothers protect their children, but Bianca has not protected Shelby, and because of that, Leslie has been questioning her own mothering all day.

'You chased him away. He's left and he won't be back. This wasn't how it was supposed to end...'

'What does that mean, Bianca? What does that mean?' shouts Randall. 'Do you know where Millie is? Do you? Because if you do... You have no idea...' He clenches a fist, raises it towards his ex-wife.

Despite her strange vision and the way her stomach is churning, despite the weakness in her legs, Leslie leaps to her feet, fuelled by adrenaline. She throws herself towards Bianca and grabs her by the shoulders, pressing her fingers hard into the plump flesh.

'You stupid, selfish woman. Tell us what you know, tell us right now. He has my child, he's taken my child and hurt your daughter, and you don't care, you don't care at all. What kind of a person are you? What kind of a mother?'

Bianca doesn't do anything, just stands there, shock on her face.

'Say something,' screams Leslie. 'Say something.' Bianca's skin is clammy, her chest heaving. Leslie squeezes her harder, wanting to make her speak – react – anything.

But Bianca pulls Leslie's hands off her body. 'This is all your fault,' she says, staring at her daughter, hatred in her eyes. 'All your fault.' She turns and leaves the room, and as they stand in stunned silence, they hear the front door slam and Bianca's car screech off.

'Oh God,' says Randall. He slumps down onto Shelby's bed. 'I'm so sorry, sweetheart. I had no idea, no idea what you were dealing with. You won't stay here. You'll come home with us.'

This is madness, just madness. How did I not know what was going on?'

'I didn't tell you, Dad,' says Shelby.

Leslie looks at her stepdaughter and sees that the child is sitting up on her bed now. She feels her knees sag, and she slides down onto the carpet, her back against the wall. 'Please, Shelby...' she whispers.

Shelby stands up. 'You better call Constable Dickerson, Dad. He needs to hear this.' Her voice is strong, her shoulders back, and there is a determined look on her face. To Leslie, she sounds older than she did this morning. Something has changed. Something is broken or something has been fixed, she is not sure which.

Randall nods his head, takes out his phone and calls the constable. 'Dickerson here,' they all hear as he puts the phone on speaker.

'Constable Dickerson,' he says. 'I'm at my ex-wife's house. Trevor has left and I think Bianca has gone after him. Leslie received an email from... someone, we have no idea who, but it showed an article and it was about Trevor. Look on her computer. He had something to do with what happened to Millie. Leslie is hurt but okay, and Shelby wants to tell us what happened. We have to listen... Please, we have to listen.'

'This is most unusual. We've been searching for you for the last half an hour. Neither of you has answered your phone and I now have people looking for the two of you as well as your daughter. You've caused a lot of trouble and—'

'You're right, Constable Dickerson, absolutely right, but please listen to me and maybe that will help you find my little sister,' interrupts Shelby. She folds her arms and stares down at the phone as though the policeman can see her.

'Right – go ahead. I'm sending people over there right now. Tell us what happened, Shelby.'

'Yesterday afternoon...' Shelby begins.

CHAPTER THIRTY-FIVE
SHELBY

'... Mum must have told him I was alone with Millie,' says Shelby.

'But how did Mum know?' asks Randall.

'She always calls me like a million time when I'm at yours,' she says, rubbing her hand across her forehead in frustration. 'She asks a hundred questions about what I'm eating and where you and Leslie are and things like that, and when I tell her I'm babysitting, she always tells me that you're taking advantage of me. I kind of agree with her, but not because I really agree. She doesn't like to hear that I'm happy with you and I understand that. It's hard for her. I was really pleased when she met Trevor. When they were dating, he was nice, but he didn't really talk to me. It only started when they got married. I kept thinking that I was getting it wrong, but now...' She bites her lips and sniffs, a tear falling from her face to her neck.

'I wish you had told me,' says her father. 'I wish you had just said. I would have believed you, Shelby, I would have helped.'

'Sorry,' comes Constable Dickerson's voice. 'Are you saying he touches you, that he's inappropriate with you?'

Shelby shivers, wipes her face roughly. 'Yeah, he... I don't know how to explain it,' she says.

'Right, no worries, go on.' The constable's voice is firm, and she feels he makes it that way so that she'll keep talking, so she'll get the facts straight and not just dissolve into a puddle of embarrassed tears, because she might just do that. Feelings of anger rise up, of pain, of sadness, but overwhelming them all is this terrible feeling of humiliation. She is exposing something gross to her father and Leslie, and even worse than that, there is another man listening on the phone. A policeman, but still a man, and if Shelby had the chance, she would pull the covers over her head and disappear. But she can't do that now. This is not just about her.

'He made me think that I was getting it all wrong and I believed him most of the time, I believed him, but I...' Her cheeks are wet with tears, but she cannot give in to tears now. She has to explain. 'On Saturday when I was babysitting Millie, Kiera came over...'

'Kiera?' asks the constable.

'She's a friend of Shelby's,' says her dad, 'but I don't—'

'Right, let's just allow Shelby to finish speaking,' says the constable. Randall nods and is silent, as though the constable is in the room with them.

'Millie wanted us to draw with her but Kiera didn't want to and...' Shelby waves her hands. There is too much to explain and she feels like she can't speak quickly enough. 'Millie got cross and said she would run away, and Kiera opened the door and told her to go, and she did and we chased her and then she ran into the road...'

'Oh God,' says Leslie.

'But she didn't get hit,' says Shelby quickly, 'she didn't. She was fine, but the car she ran in front of was Trevor's, and he got out and yelled at me and Kiera ran away, and then he followed us into the house. Millie was fine. She was fine, but then he got us both some juice and he... sat down next to me...'

'Shelby, please, where is she? Where is my baby?' whispers Leslie, and Shelby can see that something is very wrong with her stepmother. She is kind of crouched on the floor, and her skin is pale against her black hair, her brown eyes big in her face, with dark shadows underneath.

She has to explain it all in order, so she keeps going. 'He put his arm around my shoulders and then he looked at Millie and said, "She's going to be a beauty when she gets older, isn't she?" That made me feel sick because of... just because he said it in kind of a creepy way. I got up to move away from him, I was going to take Millie upstairs, but he grabbed my arm and said, "Come here. Sit down and be friendly." He pulled me back down onto the sofa and I sat because I didn't want Millie to get scared. She had stopped colouring and she was watching us really closely.'

'Millie, Millie, Millie...' moans Leslie softly to herself, and Shelby is filled with regret and sadness at what she is going to say, at what she is going to tell this woman about her child.

She can't sit still for a moment longer. Nerves jangle and jump inside her. They are going to blame her. They are not going to blame her. They are going to blame her. They are not going to blame her. She stands up and starts pacing around the room, talking, but looking at her feet in their stripy pink and purple socks. She cannot bear to look at anyone as she tells them what happened.

'He put his arms around me and he kind of stroked my shoulder...' She stops speaking, remembering how everywhere he touched was suddenly hot and pin-pricky, remembering his hot breath smelling of coffee in her ear, remembering the way her heart thudded inside her.

'Please, Shelby, tell us... tell us...' whispers her father. She looks at him and she can see that he's going to cry, he's actually going to cry for her. He doesn't just love Millie; he loves her as well.

'He said something like "Your mum has been so happy since we got married." And I said, "I know," but then he shook his head and told me that there was one thing still making her unhappy, and I asked him what it was and he said... he said, "It's that you and I don't seem to be getting along, that we don't seem friendly, and that makes her so sad." His one hand was on my leg, kind of stroking it, and he asked me if I remembered how sad she was before she met him, and he told me that he didn't want her to have to feel like that again because he and I couldn't get along.'

'Bastard, bastard, bastard,' whispers her father. She wishes she could stop now, but she can't, she needs to tell it all.

'I said, "Please stop," but his hand just kept going up my leg. I tried to pull away, but he held me closer. "Don't scare your little sister," he said. "Relax. I know you want your mum to be happy." He told me that he was trying so hard to make us into a real family so Mum could be happy all the time, and I was making it hard for both of them because I was so difficult.'

Her face is so hot, it burns. This is so disgusting, so wrong, so awful, but it's nearly done now, nearly over. The words keep coming as she stares at her socks on the wood floor, pink and purple, pink and purple. Nearly over. Nearly done. Nearly over, nearly done.

'I started crying then because his hand was touching me... touching me, and it was so gross,' she says, 'and I told him, "Stop, please stop. Stop!"' She feels her body trembling like it did as he sat next to her, holding her by her shoulders, his hand near places it shouldn't be. And the worst thing was that even though she had asked him to stop, had actually begged him to stop, she was already worried about him telling her mother that he was leaving because Shelby wasn't nice to him, and she knew that then her mother would be sad forever.

'Millie stood up from her chair,' she continues, and her voice is low because she feels so sad, so sad that her body feels heavy, 'and she said, "Shelby said stop and Shelby's the boss because Mum isn't home so you have to stop."'

She sees her little sister's face, filled with determination as she wagged one small finger at Trevor. And she knows that in that moment, in that few seconds of time, she loved her more than any other human being in the world, because Millie was listening to her. She was actually listening to Shelby, and it felt like no one listened to her any more. No one except Millie. But then... but then...

CHAPTER THIRTY-SIX

RUTH

I have it wrong. I see that. I only saw the end this afternoon because I couldn't look before. I have it very, very wrong. I have made a terrible, terrible mistake. 'Oh no,' I groan, rocking on my sofa. 'Oh no.'

I don't know what I'm going to do now. I don't know how I'm going to solve this problem. I return to my childhood bedroom, where everything is silent and safe, silent and safe, and I pull all the teddy bears off the bookshelf. I start counting as I replace them, waiting for my heart to slow, for my breathing to even out – waiting for a way to fix this to present itself.

CHAPTER THIRTY-SEVEN

LESLIE

12.30 a.m.

Leslie feels a sob catch in her throat at the words she always uses when she leaves Shelby with Millie. 'Shelby is the boss, Millie, until I come home, so you have to do what she says.'

'Okay, Mum, okay.'

Her little girl was excited this morning. She liked it when it was just her and Shelby in the house. Leslie tries to limit junk food, as every mother does, but she knows that when it is just Shelby and Millie at home together, Shelby will allow Millie to have more treats than she should have. She knows this, but she ignores it, because sisters need to have secrets, sisters need to bond over besting the adults in their lives, even if it's over something as small as sneaking junk food. She has been hoping, since Millie was born, that her little girl and Shelby will be close enough that one day, long after she and Randall are gone, Millie will have someone to turn to.

'I told Millie to sit down,' continues Shelby, her voice getting softer as she stares down at her socks. Leslie holds her breath, not wanting to hear what's coming next, not wanting to know, not wanting to feel what she's going to have to feel. 'But she didn't sit down. She came to stand right next to me and she was holding those little playdough scissors in her hand – you know, from that set you bought her?'

Leslie nods, knowing exactly which scissors Shelby is talking about. They're a reddy-orange colour and only able to cut the coloured dough Millie likes to shape and mould. Millie knows that scissors, real scissors, can be dangerous. She's not allowed to touch the real scissors in the kitchen.

Shelby goes on. 'She said, "Stop, leave Shelby alone," and she tried to climb on my lap. Trevor yelled at her to get off, and he pushed her, just pushed, and she fell onto the floor and just kind of lay there, but her eyes were open and she was looking at me. She was fine, but then he shoved his hand really high and it hurt and I shouted, "Ow," and Millie jumped up and grabbed his hair.'

Shelby stops speaking and looks at them. 'I tried to stop him,' she says. 'I'm so sorry.' And then she sinks onto the floor, sobbing. 'He threw her off, and her head...' She touches the back of her own head, and Leslie feels a sharp pain where she knows Millie's head hit the table. 'There was a sound, like a clunk, and she fell on the floor and just lay there,' whispers Shelby. 'She just lay there with her eyes closed and she wasn't moving, she wasn't moving...' Her sobs are loud in the room, a burst dam, emotions rushing out, fear and shame and anger and pain everywhere, filling the air.

Randall, his face pale with horror, goes over to his daughter and wraps his arms around her. 'Shh,' he says, 'shh, it's okay... it's okay.'

But it's not okay.

Leslie watches the two of them, feeling apart, feeling separate and alone, and even though she knows this should bother

her, it doesn't. She *is* alone. Completely alone, and that is how it should be.

Millie is gone. Leslie knows this with certainty. Her little girl, her darling child, is gone.

CHAPTER THIRTY-EIGHT

SHELBY

She stops crying, stands up and pulls away from her father so she can grab a tissue from her bedside table.

'Right, Shelby, and what happened then?' says the constable. Shelby startles at the sound of his voice. She had forgotten he was on the phone. She takes a deep breath.

'He picked her up and she was... just lying in his arms, and her eyes were closed. And he said, "This is your fault. Your stupid bloody fault. You did this, Shelby. You." He kind of looked around like he didn't know what to do, and then he said, "Leave the front door open. Tell them she ran away. Tell them you came downstairs from the... from the bathroom and she was gone, and keep your mouth shut. I'm warning you, keep your mouth shut." Then he left.'

She lets the last of Trevor's words hang in the air, in the silence where she can feel her stepmother's deep despair, her father's utter incomprehension, her own terrible guilt.

She remembers how she stood there in the living room once Trevor had run out of the front door, just stood there with cold air blowing in, frozen on the spot. She had no idea how what had just happened had happened, but as her muscles started to cramp, she knew one thing for sure. She would be blamed. It was her fault, and even if she tried to tell people about Trevor, no one would believe her. No one. Who believes a child over an adult?

She had wanted to sink onto the sofa, to cry for her little sister, to scream and rage, but she ran upstairs, her bladder nearly bursting with anxiety and fear, and she used the bathroom, and then she went back down and for some reason she called for Millie, she called for her little sister as though nothing had happened and she might, might just be there, sitting at her little table, her crayon in her hand, a smile on her face. She picked up the glasses of juice and took them to the kitchen, thinking Millie might be in there, her hand in the treat jar. And then she rinsed the glasses out and put them in the dishwasher and stood in the quiet kitchen where Millie wasn't, in the house where Millie wasn't, in the space where Millie would never be again. Only when all she felt, all she heard was the terrible, silent emptiness of the house did she start crying, and then she had called Leslie as her hysteria rose inside her and she accepted what had happened.

'I'm sorry,' she whispers finally, when it seems like the silence might go on forever.

'Okay,' comes the constable's voice, and everyone in the room stares at the phone as though he has the answer, he knows what to do. 'While you've been talking, I've indicated to my colleague that we need to find this Trevor Richards, or Tony Richardson, whoever he is. Constable Willow has found the email you've mentioned and we're tracing it. You need to come back here, please. The car should be there now.'

In Shelby's window, red and blue lights flash as the police car pulls into the driveway.

'We need a statement from Shelby. I'll alert everyone now. I need to find his car rego and then we will get him. I promise you we will get him. Please return to the house.'

'Okay,' says her dad. 'Okay.' His voice is flat and sad, his shoulders hunched. He looks... broken. Shelby has broken her father and her stepmother, slumped on the floor. She has broken them.

CHAPTER THIRTY-NINE

RUTH

As I put the last teddy bear on the shelf, I know what I have to do. It is nearly one in the morning, another day, but I know what I have to do.

I take one teddy bear off the shelf and put it on the bed, covering it with my grandmother's blanket. 'Safe,' I whisper, and then I dress in my layers and take my bag filled with stones and I leave the house, leaving the lights on, knowing I need to be very, very quick. I climb into my car and I am on my way to right my mistake, on my way to tell the truth – to let the mother know, to let her know everything.

CHAPTER FORTY

LESLIE

12.45 a.m.

'How are we going to find her?' asks Leslie. 'How are we ever going to find her... even just her...' She doesn't say the word, refuses to say the word 'body', though she is certain now that this is what they are looking for, all the searchers and the police.

'We need to get back to the house,' Randall says, and he holds his hand towards Leslie so that she can grab it, which she does. He pulls her up off the floor and wraps his arms around her for a brief, tight moment. She rests her head against his chest, hearing the steady beat of his heart, knowing that her own heart is beating too, even though surely it must stop now. If her baby girl is gone, she cannot possibly still be here. But here she is.

Her head has cleared, even as the headache holds tight. She feels like a drunk person, sobered by shock. She is a hurt person, sobered by despair.

She feels rather than sees Shelby come to stand next to them, and she turns her head and looks at her stepchild, at this girl who has only been in her life for five years. Shelby is hunched and pale and she wraps her arms around herself as though she has no hope of comfort from anyone else. She is a child who has been betrayed in a way a child should never be betrayed, her sister is probably dead, and her mother has chosen to go after the man who has tortured her for the last six months instead of staying with her only daughter. Leslie is unsure who Shelby will become after this, who they all will be. She lets go of Randall and steps back a little, then she turns and opens her arms to her stepdaughter.

'It wasn't your fault,' she whispers. 'It wasn't your fault.'

Shelby steps into her arms and folds herself into them, her head on Leslie's shoulder, and then Randall's arms surround them both. Leslie knows in this moment that she has lost her daughter but also that she still has a daughter. She still has Shelby.

Finally the three of them part and Randall wipes his eyes with his shirt. 'We need to get back now,' he says. 'Pack up some stuff, Shelby. No matter what happens, you are never coming back here. We'll get everything later, but just take what you need for now.'

Shelby nods and quickly stuffs her school things into her school bag and takes some books and extra clothes. The doorbell rings and Constable Willow is standing there. He doesn't speak, just nods. And then they are in the car on the way back to the house, where there are police and neighbours and those trying to help, but nothing they do will be enough. Millie is gone. She is gone forever.

CHAPTER FORTY-ONE

SHELBY

It is so late, so quiet, the streets so empty. The police car cruises through dark streets where other people live. Other people are warm and safe in their beds. She will never have to go back, and if they try to make her, she will refuse.

She cannot think about her mother's betrayal now, cannot believe that she chose to run after Trevor. All that matters is finding Millie, finding her sister.

She will think about what her mother has done later... what her mother knows.

'I think,' she says aloud, 'I think Mum knows what happened. I think she does. I heard her on the phone to him and I think she knows.' She is certain of this now, certain in that terrible way that she is certain her little sister is gone, certain in the awful way she is certain her mother chose an evil man over her. She is certain.

'Yes,' says Leslie, softly, sadly. 'I think you're right.'

Shelby stares at the street lights, narrowing her eyes a little, creating one long whizzing yellow light like she used to do as a much younger child. She was going to teach Millie how to do that. She was going to teach Millie how to paint her nails carefully and slowly. She was going to teach Millie how to deal with bullies, how to make cupcakes, what to say to a boy or girl she likes. She was going to do so many things with her little sister, because she is, she was, her little sister; not her half-sister – just her sister. And now that has been taken from her and she feels her hands become fists. She would like to kill Trevor. It's a horrible, burning, angry feeling inside her.

As they pull into the driveway of the house, Shelby is surprised that there is no press there, only Constable Dickerson pacing in the driveway.

The young constable stops the car and Constable Dickerson opens the door where her father is sitting. 'We've had a call,' he says, 'from your ex-wife.'

'She knows where Millie is,' says her father, his voice flat.

'Right. How did you...?' begins the constable. 'She called and said that she'd caught up with her husband and managed to convince him to tell her where he'd left the child.'

'That's a lie,' says her father. 'She knew where Millie was all along.'

Shelby wants to leap in to defend her mother, to say that she would never do something like that, but she knows it's the truth. What kind of a person is her mother? And what kind of a person does that make Shelby?

Her father climbs out of the car and Leslie gets out after him. 'Where is she? Where is she?' she says.

'In the park,' says Constable Dickerson. 'She said she's in the park and we have everyone there now. They're all there. But I have to tell you, I'm afraid that we've scoured the area – we had people looking all day and night – and Millie is not where Bianca said she would be. She's not there. She told us exactly where she would be and I have people there with lights, but she's not there. We'll keep looking, but we have to accept that we may have been lied to. I'm so sorry, but we will keep looking.'

'We have to go there,' says Leslie.

'Please,' says the constable. 'Please just wait here, wait here now.'

Shelby watches her stepmother sag against the car, her knees giving way, and in an instant, she is out of the car, her arms around her, supporting her. Leslie is nearly the same size she is, and so, until her father turns around to help, Shelby holds her stepmother up.

CHAPTER FORTY-TWO

RUTH

I race through the streets in my little yellow Beetle, on my way to the house where I was only yesterday, to the house I followed him to.

He was in his gym outfit, sweat marks under his arms, smelling strongly of deodorant when he came into the coffee shop. He never noticed me, never has. I am too old for Touchy Tony now, too old, but I needed to know if there was another young girl he was hurting. I wanted to know who he lived with and where he lived, to know if he had a wife or a girlfriend, and finally, on Saturday, I had found the courage to follow him.

But I got some things very wrong. I thought I saw something, but I saw something entirely different. Touchy Tony is now Trevor and he is not the child's father. I have made a terrible, terrible mistake. I followed him from the coffee shop, followed his car, and I was a few car lengths behind him when the child darted out into the road and he screeched on his brakes. I was able to stop too, and I watched, my heart in my mouth, as he got out of the car and yelled at the teenager following the little girl. I pulled to the side of the road and they didn't notice me, because they were so involved in their own drama. I didn't expect him to follow them into the house. And I thought he had done it, had pulled his car into the driveway and followed her in, because it was his house, his large, looming mansion.

He had been so angry with the older girl that I thought, perhaps he is her father, perhaps he is the father of both girls, although they didn't look like sisters.

I waited for my body to calm down from the shock of seeing the child in the road. I waited a long time as I studied the house with its neat front garden and I could see that he had done very well for himself, that he had everything including two daughters. Karma had not punished Touchy Tony – he had been rewarded. He had run away again and again and each time he had been rewarded. I wondered, my stomach churning, if he did to them what he had done to me, to all the other girls he had taught.

I sat there for some time, and I was just about to turn my car around, to take my anger at his good luck home with me, when he came out of the house again with the little girl, the small child, limp in his arms. And I knew, I just knew, that he had done something terrible, something that could not be denied, and I had seen him. The world is full of nasty coincidences. Although I had been watching him, following him, waiting and hoping to see him do something that would allow me to expose him to the world, now that it was here, all I could feel was horror at the limp body in his arms.

I watched him get into his car, shoving the child carelessly into the back seat, his movements panicked and frantic.

'Oh,' I moaned aloud, 'oh no.' He had hurt the child; I knew he had.

I followed him, keeping my eyes on his silver car, followed him as he circled the block once and then as he made his way towards the park.

He went down a side road that ran alongside the park, and I

started to follow him, but I could see that it ended in a dead end, so I pulled over.

I parked next to a house across the road from the park, behind a line of cars, noticed the balloons tied to the gate of the house. Some child was having a party. I got out of my car, stood in the street listening to joyous shouts from the back yard. 'Time for cake,' I heard a man's voice call. I couldn't see anything. I moved quickly, away from the house and towards where he had parked his car.

As I got closer, I heard his voice.

'Listen to me, just listen to me. It wasn't my fault. I was going to check on her. You don't want them to see her and I agree.' He kept talking, mentioned going to court and needing something to hold against them. I didn't know who he was talking about but I did know that his voice went from panic, quick exclaiming sentences, to calm and slow as he convinced whoever he was speaking to that she needed to believe him when he said nothing was his fault, when he told her he was a good man just trying to make her happy. It was obviously a she, a woman he was talking to. I remember the way he talked to women, to girls, a special lilt to his voice.

'You know I would do anything to make you happy. That's all that matters to me,' he said, and as he listened to the woman on the phone, I crept closer. I could see him pacing up and down next to his car. He'd pulled to the side of the road next to the park.

'I don't know why. I panicked, so I just picked her up. But what do I do now?' he said to the person on the phone. I wondered if he was talking to the little girl's mother, but then I realised that he couldn't be. A mother wouldn't let something like that happen to her child. Mothers are supposed to protect their children, unless... they don't. When I saw her on television, saw her naked grief and fear, I knew she was not the woman he was talking to. He hadn't just hurt his little girl; he was also probably having an affair. Touchy Tony – once a liar, always a liar.

I held my breath and took a few more steps. He hadn't noticed me. I was close, but the park was filled with bush where he was and it was easy enough to crouch down a little so he couldn't see me. The sky was grey and heavy and the air cold, and the only thing I could hear was someone calling for what I assumed was a dog: 'Baxter, Baxter, come on, come on, let's go, come find the ball, let's go.'

'Yeah, okay,' Tony said. 'I'm by the park. I'll leave her here, right here, good idea. She's... I don't know... yeah, she's breathing. I mean, it was just a little knock on the head... Right, right. I'll leave her here and then there'll be a search. I'll find her. I'll find her first... Okay. I love you. You need to know that I love you more than anything in the world and all I want is for you to be happy... Yeah, okay.'

I understood what he was going to do and I crouched down further until I was practically sitting on the cold ground, hidden by some bushes with prickly green leaves. I watched him lift the little body out of the car and place her on the ground, gently, carefully. He stroked her face once and I thought I saw love in the way he touched her, whatever love he was capable of. I thought he was her father.

'Okay,' he kept saying, 'okay, okay.'

I lifted my hand to my mouth and bit down on a finger to make sure I kept silent. What kind of a father was he? She was so little. He had never tried anything with someone so little before. It was sickening, but he was a sick and twisted man. He loved his daughter but he had hurt her. He had no real idea of what love was.

I waited until he got into his car, looking around, checking to see if anyone was watching. And then he just drove off, just turned his car around and drove away. Touchy Tony, Trevor Richards – getting away with it again.

He would report his own child missing, would join the search for her and then find her and be a hero. Gaslighting the whole world.

I wasn't going to let that happen.

I stood up from my hiding spot and walked towards her. Pink Ugg boots and a pale face, dark lashes and black hair and a still, still little body.

But not his daughter. Someone else's child. I should have known. He has always hurt someone else's child.

Now I arrive at the large, beautiful house, the large house that does not belong to him. I park and get out. It is that strange time of the morning when it seems only minutes away from getting light but I know it will be hours. I pull my coat around me against the spiky wind and walk towards the house, where all is silent. There is no press here now, no one to look, no one to see.

There is only me. Me and what I have seen and done, and what I have to do now.

CHAPTER FORTY-THREE

LESLIE

1.30 a.m.

She is sitting in the kitchen with a cold cup of tea. In front of her, the screen on her phone reads 1.30 a.m. Such a strange time to be awake, although she remembers the not-so-long-ago night feedings with Millie, just her and the baby in the rocking chair in her room, the whole world asleep except for the two of them, or so it seemed. To many mothers, the baby stage is the worst stage. All you have is a small, needy creature who is unable to communicate what's bothering them. But Leslie had loved it, had loved the idea that she was everything to this tiny being, that she had made her and now she got to hold her and feed her and feel her skin on hers.

Randall is lying down in their bed and Constable Dickerson is dozing on the sofa in the living room. They are all waiting for the email to be traced, hoping that the person may have seen something, may know something.

'Don't you get to go home?' she had asked the constable an hour ago.

'I'm technically off shift, but I've asked to stay. I need to stay,' he said, and then he had patted her arm lightly and she had felt his concern and care. The park has been searched completely, thoroughly and continuously. But they will not stop looking.

The television is off, but she knows they are looking for Trevor. Bianca has not made contact since her call to the police, not even to speak to her daughter. Constable Dickerson has Shelby's phone in case she calls. The police know she has concealed what Trevor did, although she may try to argue that she found out at the same time as everyone else. But she had left by then, run off after Trevor, after her man. She definitely knew that he had left Millie in the park. Why else would she point the police in that direction? But Millie is still missing, still gone. She is not in the park, not anywhere. It feels impossible and yet it's reality. Did Bianca also know that Trevor was being inappropriate with her daughter? Did she know but not want to know? Leslie shudders at the thought of a man, any man, touching her child that way. It's sick.

She lifts her hand to touch the back of her head, feeling the growing lump there. She has cleaned away the blood but has refused to go to the hospital until her child is found. She hadn't protested or argued, simply refused. And Randall and Constable Dickerson have accepted this.

She hears what she thinks is a soft knock at the front door, and her body stiffens, her breath catching, because she's not entirely sure she's heard anything, but then it comes again and she gets up to go to the door, knowing she has only heard it because the rest of the house is so quiet. She has a brief lift in her heart at the thought that it might be her little girl returning home. Millie is too small to ring the bell. But she knows it's not.

Realising she should probably wake the constable in case she needs him, Leslie opens the door anyway.

Standing on the step is a woman in a baggy green dress,

skinny, with brown curly hair streaked with grey, held back by a large clip.

'Yes?' says Leslie, wary in case she's a journalist.

'You're her mother,' says the woman, her voice soft and low.

'Yes,' says Leslie, and she takes a step back, ready to close the door in the strange woman's face, ready to shout for the constable and run.

'You look like her,' says the woman, and then she clears her throat.

Leslie knows that she should slam the door. The woman has seen what happened on television and is here in some kind of strange voyeuristic way to see the mother of a missing child in real life. But maybe because of the late hour, or because of the silence, or because her exhaustion is making her feel slightly woozy as she deals with the knock she took to her head, Leslie just stands there and she and the woman look at each other.

'I can take you to her,' says the woman.

'What?' Leslie gasps.

'My name is Ruth,' says the woman, calm and controlled, 'and I can take you to her.' She has her hand in her bag and she seems to be touching something, and Leslie thinks it may be a gun – why not? Anything is possible – but then she pulls her hand out of her bag and shows Leslie a shiny black stone. 'Tourmaline for protection,' she says. 'I don't... I can take you to her. Please. I can.'

Leslie stares at her open-mouthed, rooted to the spot. The silence in the house grows to envelop her, the slightly orange sky a strange backdrop to the woman, making Leslie think she's hallucinating.

'Do you understand?' asks Ruth, and she leans forward and touches Leslie lightly on the arm, forcing her to jerk back, shock whirling through her body. The woman is real. What she has said is real.

'Randall, Randall...' shouts Leslie, but she doesn't move, still afraid the woman is an apparition and she is seeing and hearing things. She keeps her eye on the stranger who stands at the front door. Ruth looks calm, but when Leslie glances at her hands, at the way she is opening and closing one of them in some sort of compulsive way as she uses the other to stroke the stone in her bag, she realises that the woman is afraid.

'What is it?' asks Constable Dickerson, coming to the front door.

'Les, Les, are you okay?' she hears Randall saying as he comes down the stairs, his glasses in his hand, his clothes rumpled from sleep.

'She says...' begins Leslie, and then she stops, terrified for a moment that she is going to be told she is staring at nothing, that there is not a woman standing at her door telling her she can take her to her child.

'Right, can I have your name, please?' says Constable Dickerson, fully in police mode.

'It's Ruth,' says the woman. 'I can take you to her. You come in my car with me,' she says to Leslie. 'They can follow.' And then she turns and walks away, towards a yellow Beetle parked in the street.

Leslie looks at Randall and Constable Dickerson.

'What?' says Randall.

'Just wait a minute,' the constable calls to the woman.

'You can follow,' says Leslie, and it is only after she has run from the house even as Randall tried to grab her that she remembers she is wearing her fluffy pink slippers instead of shoes.

'Leslie, wait,' she hears.

'You can follow,' she shouts as the woman climbs into her car and waits for Leslie. 'You can follow.'

Later she will think of this moment and know that what she did was ridiculous and dangerous. She put herself and everyone around her in danger. Without knowing who she was getting into a car with, she simply did it, and later she will wonder at herself, at her choice. But in the moment, in this moment, she is absolutely certain that this woman knows where her child is. It's not a thought; more a feeling, a knowing, a deep, intense knowing. This woman will take her to her child.

What dawns on her as they drive the silent streets, only their breathing making any sound in the car, is that this is what she has been dreading all day, all night. Millie was missing but now she is found, and if the woman did not simply bring her to the door, it is because she is no longer alive. She was missing but now she is found, and Leslie will be forever utterly, utterly lost.

CHAPTER FORTY-FOUR

SHELBY

She is curled up on her bed when she hears the shouting, and she sits up immediately, knowing that something has happened, aware that it's not good. Despair settles over her. This is how she will feel forever. She will never have to see Trevor again, will struggle to talk to her mother, and her little sister is gone. Have they found her? Have they found her body?

She climbs off the bed, shivering in the cold air without her blanket, and opens her bedroom door. 'It's fine,' says a woman constable who must have replaced the other constable, the young man. 'It's fine.'

'What's happening?' Shelby asks.

'They think...' the woman begins, and then she stops, obviously wondering if she should tell Shelby anything.

'They've found her,' says Shelby, her voice a whisper, lost in the sadness of it all.

'They think so,' says the constable. Shelby wants to run downstairs, where all the lights are on, wants to find her father, but she finds her feet are too heavy to go far. Instead, she turns and goes back to her bed, pulling the soft blanket over her head and curling up small.

'Are you hiding, Shelby?' she hears her little sister say.

'Yes,' she whispers to the ghost. 'I'm hiding.'

CHAPTER FORTY-FIVE

RUTH

We drive in silence. I have so much to tell her, so many things to say, such a lot to explain, but I cannot think how to begin. She is the first person who has sat in the passenger seat of my car since my mother died. The only other person, in fact. I have been alone all my life because of him. I have never had a good friend or a lover. I am a middle-aged woman and he has taken everything from me. I could have had a life, I know that. But it wasn't just him. It was everyone around him, and the way they made me question and doubt myself.

'How did you find her?' she whispers. She is a pretty woman, delicate and small, with lovely hair, just like her little girl.

'I saw him,' I say.

'Him?' she questions.

'Tony... I mean Trevor. I've been... It's a long story, but I've been following him and I saw him leave your house with her. He was carrying her.'

'Why have you been following him?'

'I knew him when I was a teenager.'

'Right, he was a teacher,' she says, her voice devoid of any interest, just stating a fact.

'Yes,' I say, 'but there's more to it than that. Here we are.' I pull into the driveway of my small house and experience a brief moment of worry about what she will think of my home, and then I realise that she will not care at all. There is only one thing she wants to see.

The police car with her husband in pulls up behind us. 'Quickly,' I say, needing to be inside before they try and stop us.

She gets out and we both dart up the path to the front door.

When I open the door, I turn to her and say, 'I'm sorry. I thought Tony... Trevor was your husband. I thought she was his child. I was wrong.'

She nods, silent, impatient, despairing.

I take her to the back of the house, leading her on a strange, wavy route around all my piles. I hear an intake of breath at what she sees, but she doesn't comment. I open the bedroom door, where all is still and silent. She stands in the doorway for a moment, her body frozen. She is afraid. I understand.

And then she walks in and over to the bed, where she drops to her knees. The little girl has not moved since I laid her down there. I should have taken her to the hospital, I know I should have. But I couldn't let her go back to him. I had to make sure that everyone knew it was him. The mistakes have piled up, and as I watch the woman, I understand that what I have done today is mad. I have been slightly mad since I saw him in the coffee shop, since I started following him, since I witnessed him leave her body in the park. I have been mad, and now I can see that my life, however terrible it was, is about to get worse. I will be blamed for this. At school, when I tried to tell the guidance counsellor, he blamed me. 'You're making up this nonsense,' he told me. At home, when I tried to explain to my mother, she blamed me. 'Something is very wrong with you, Ruth.' And now that I have tried to tell the world, they will blame me for keeping her, and that is ultimately completely my fault.

She lifts her hand and places it on her little girl's chest, and I can hear her murmuring softly, 'Oh baby, oh my baby, oh my darling.' She is touching her chest, something I couldn't bring myself to do. I did cover her with my blanket, and tucked one of my soft teddy bears in next to her to keep her safe. I made sure she was warm, but I didn't know if she was still alive. When I picked her up, I felt her breathing; when I placed her gently in my car, I felt the warmth in her body. When I brought her into my house, I felt her filling the air with her spirit. But I have been afraid to check on her too closely. I should have done that, should have rushed her to hospital and called the police.

But what if they had blamed me? I tried to explain when I was younger, tried to tell everyone what he was doing, but they asked so many questions, pointed out inconsistencies, made me repeat myself so I made mistakes. I understood that where he was involved, I would always be the one to blame. I didn't want that to happen to his little girl. I didn't think he deserved a little girl. But she's not his little girl.

I feel like I have suddenly woken up. What have I done?

The woman's eyes widen and she looks at me, horror or something else on her face. I feel the two men behind me, and she opens her mouth and screams.

CHAPTER FORTY-SIX

LESLIE

2.00 a.m.

'She's still breathing,' screams Leslie. 'She's still breathing.' Her hands on her baby girl's chest, she can feel the slight, almost imperceptible rise of her chest. Her skin is pale and her body is still, but she is alive. She is breathing.

Randall is immediately beside her, and he touches his daughter as Leslie watches him, willing him to see the same thing, to notice the same thing. And then Constable Dickerson is next to the bed as well, his fingers on Millie's little neck as he checks for a pulse while summoning an ambulance on his radio.

'Just get here now!' he barks.

It seems only moments until sirens ring through the air, whirling lights bounce off the windows and the paramedics arrive, filling the room with a cold wind. Randall hauls Leslie away from the bed so they can get to their child.

They stand in the corner and Leslie feels her stomach turn and her legs go weak. 'Please, please...' she begs.

'Let's go,' says a woman paramedic, nodding at Leslie and Randall, and Leslie can see that Millie's face is covered with an oxygen mask. Finally it's real, finally it's confirmed. Whatever happens from here, her daughter is alive right now. She is alive.

'The mother,' shouts the woman paramedic, and Leslie pulls away from Randall and runs after them, because she is the mother, will always be the mother, and her baby girl is alive.

CHAPTER FORTY-SEVEN

SHELBY

Her father only returns from the hospital after the sun has been up for hours, the house warmed by winter sunshine, the front garden, filled with trampled flower beds, holding the memory of all the people who had come to see, to ask, to help.

She has not slept all night long, needing to stay awake until she knew her sister was safe. The policewoman had come into her room to tell her that Millie was on the way to the hospital.

'But she's...' Shelby had said, and then she had not managed the word 'dead'.

'She's alive,' the constable said, and Shelby had to dart for the bathroom and use the toilet as the word spun around in her brain. Alive, alive, alive. She had not been dead when Trevor picked up her floppy body and carried it out of the house, hissing, 'Tell them she ran away.'

When her father comes into the house, she is sitting on the sofa, wrapped in a blanket, a cup of hot chocolate in her hands, made for her by the constable, who is sweet and kind and who has not asked any questions, has just sat with her as they waited. Now she is so tired she could cry, but she can't sleep. She's not allowed to close her eyes until she knows if her sister is okay.

She hears him call 'thank you' to whoever has dropped him off, another policeman probably, and she waits, tense and filled with fear, until he comes in and slumps onto the sofa. 'Thanks,' he says to the policewoman, who nods and stands up. Shelby realises that she has actually been babysitting her as well, and feels her cheeks colour at the thought that she still needs a babysitter, but at the same time she is grateful that the police-woman was here. She has been sitting quietly with her since two in the morning, watching as Shelby flicked through televi-sion channels where old sitcoms and people selling jewellery and vacuum cleaners seemed to be the only things on, until the morning shows and the news, where the story was everywhere, Millie's face, their house, Trevor on repeat. Police were looking for him, searching for Trevor Richards, also known as Tony Richardson, in connection with kidnapping and grievous bodily harm of a child under ten, and numerous incidents of sexual assault and harassment. They also mentioned they were looking for an unidentified woman, and Shelby knew that was her mother. Concealing a crime is a crime.

She remembered meeting Trevor for the first time after her mother had been dating him for a few weeks. They met on an online dating site and her mother was always sure to make it clear that she was a single mother. Was that why Trevor had liked her – chosen her? This thought disgusted Shelby. But he had seemed so ordinary the first time she met him, just some man who made her mother laugh. Only after they were married, after the small wedding where her mother's dress was just a little too tight, did the man he was become apparent. But every time Shelby thought about saying something, about saying it directly and clearly, she had watched her mother talking or laughing with Trevor and she had thought, she's so happy. You can't destroy that.

Now it feels like the worst thing is that her mother knew all along where Millie was, knew what Trevor had done, and had made a choice – had chosen one person over her own daughter, over her ex-husband's daughter, over everyone else.

Her mother has not contacted her, and even if she had, Shelby wouldn't know. The police have her phone just in case she does. Not having her phone makes Shelby feel strange, but also a little relieved. She doesn't want to have to respond to the endless messages that she knows are filling up her DMs, and she also has no idea what she would say to her mother if she did call her. She doesn't want to speak to her, not now and maybe not ever again.

Her father takes his glasses off and cleans them, something Shelby knows he does when he needs some time, and she gives him that by keeping quiet, her mind slowing now that he is here, her body relaxing.

When he puts his glasses down on the coffee table, Shelby moves closer to him on the sofa. She takes half of the blanket she has wrapped around herself and covers his legs. His face is pale, his eyes bloodshot, and he carries the disinfectant smell of the hospital on his clothes.

'I'll see myself out. Try to rest,' says the policewoman to both of them, and her father nods his head.

'Thanks,' he says again.

They wait while she leaves, closing the door quietly behind her.

'Tell me, Dad,' begs Shelby then. 'Tell me how she is.'

He sighs. 'She has a concussion. If she'd got to the hospital sooner, it would have been okay, but there is some bleeding on her brain. It may resolve by itself or they may have to operate, and so they don't...' he hunches over, his hands covering his face, 'don't know if she'll be okay.'

His shoulders heave and Shelby knows he's crying, and the sick feeling she has carried with her since it happened rises in her throat. She covers her mouth with her hand and swallows fast. 'It's my—' she begins to say.

'Don't say that,' he yells, sitting up and wiping his eyes. 'Don't you ever say that, Shelby. It's *our* fault. My fault and your mother's fault. We didn't protect you from him. We should have seen something, should have asked questions, but we were so wrapped up in ourselves that we didn't. It's our fault, Shelby. You're just a kid and you should get to be a kid.'

Even though her father is yelling at her, even though he seems angry, Shelby allows the words to comfort her, to settle inside her so she can believe them. Every day has been hard for the last six months, and she wanted to, really wanted to tell someone – anyone – what was happening, but she couldn't because she was afraid. Afraid she wouldn't be believed. Afraid she was making it up. Afraid it was all her fault. Afraid of hurting her mother.

But it wasn't her fault, it isn't, and all she can hope for, pray for is that Millie is okay and that one day, a long time from now, this will all feel like a really bad dream.

She doesn't know if they will find Trevor and put him in prison for hurting Millie, and for doing to the girls he taught the same disgusting things he was doing to her, but he's out of her life now and that's all that matters.

Her mother is a different story.

She is too tired to think about her mother now.

Her father leans back and sighs, closes his eyes, and Shelby moves closer to him again and puts her head on his shoulder. He lifts his arm and wraps it around her shoulders, holding her tight, keeping her safe, and together they sleep.

CHAPTER FORTY-EIGHT

RUTH

'Miss Thornton, I know we've been over this again and again, but do you think you could explain it to us one more time?' says the detective. I nod my head, because I don't mind telling him again. I know what they are looking for – inconsistencies. They also want to know why, and I have been dancing around that. It's my story and they don't need to know everything.

Outside, the sun has come up and I wonder if it will be a warm day or if it will carry the final tinge of winter in the air. I am used to being inside, but now that I have to be here, to stay here, I yearn for the outside. But I must answer their questions. It's only fair. I did the wrong thing. I thought I was doing the right thing, but... but...

'I recognised him in a coffee shop,' I say. 'I hadn't seen him for more than twenty years and I couldn't believe it. And then I just...'

'Started following him,' says the detective, who is a tall, thin man with a large Roman nose. There is a female detective sitting next to him, but she hasn't said anything. She nods her head when I speak, and writes things down even though they are recording this. But she has nice brown eyes and I can see that she feels some sympathy for me. Every now and again she gets up and brings me another cup of coffee with two sugars and full-cream milk to help me get through the endless questions. I want to go home and sleep for days, but I am not sure I'm going to be allowed to go home at all. I should have taken the child to the hospital immediately. I should never have kept her from her family, even if I thought that family was Touchy Tony – or Trevor, as he is now known. But I can't go back in time, so there is no point in dwelling on it.

'Are you going to send me to prison?' I ask the female detective.

'You will be charged with a number of offences, but it's up to a judge. Once we have finished here, a public defender will be appointed for you and then you can apply for bail. Unless you have a lawyer you want us to contact?' A small smile. She wishes it could be different – perhaps because she is a woman and understands what I have suffered.

My eyes feel hot and I squeeze them shut, hoping to avoid crying. 'I understand,' I say. 'I don't have a lawyer.' The truth is, I don't have anyone, and I have made that my choice. I have kept myself safe by keeping myself away from the whole world.

'And what were you hoping to achieve by following him?' the detective asks.

'I don't know that I was hoping to achieve anything,' I tell him. 'I just wanted to... I don't know,' I mumble. I am not sure what I would have done if he had spotted me, if he had spoken to me, recognised me. But I think it would have felt a lot like it did when I was a child. The feeling of having no control, of being frozen in place and filled with horrifying fear and disgust would have returned.

'Have you found him?' I ask instead of answering his question.

'No, but we're hopeful.'

'Australia is a big place,' I say. 'He could be anywhere.

When he disappeared from my life, I didn't see him for decades.'

'We're hopeful,' he repeats.

'Are you going to be interviewing all his past students? Because you should. There will be a lot of them that he...'

'We will be,' says the female detective. 'Calls have already started coming in since the news picked up the story. Lots of calls.'

'Sorry,' says the detective, rubbing his eyes, 'how old were you when you were in his class?'

'I was thirteen when he taught me, thirteen. He taught geography and computer science, but he never noticed me until my mother went to see him about what I had told her he was doing to the other girls. He never noticed me, but then he did.' It was so much better when I was beneath his notice, when I was too thin, too plain, too me. No one wants to be invisible, but sometimes invisible is the best you can hope for.

'Right, and so he taught you for one or two... how many years?' the detective asks.

'Only one, but I could have handled school. I would have been fine if not for...'

'If not for what?' asks the female detective, and I realise that in all the questions and all the talking we have done, I have neglected to mention this one point, this one very important point.

'If not for the fact that I became his stepchild,' I say, and both detectives sit back in their chairs.

'Sorry, are you saying he was your stepfather?' asks the female detective – I think her name is Marci, but my brain is fuzzy with exhaustion.

'For a short time.' I nod. 'After my mother went to speak to him, she came home and told me to stop saying terrible things about him, to stop lying. And then he pulled me aside and told me we should be friends and...' I stop speaking for a moment, needing to get things in order. I remember the day he pulled up alongside me in his car and offered me a lift home. I knew I shouldn't have climbed into the car with him, but I was so close to home and he was my teacher and you don't say no to a teacher. At least I didn't. And things would still have been fine then. He put his hand on my leg and slid it up a little and I crossed my legs and he removed his hand. He was so good at pulling back just before it became something that could not be explained away. But when we got to my house, he parked and told me he'd walk me to the door. I told him not to worry and thanked him for the lift, but he followed me anyway. My mother heard me open the door with my key and came to greet me, and twittered with joy when she saw him, invited him to dinner, brought out a nice bottle of wine. He was there for hours, and finally I went to bed and left them to their jokes and their laughter. In my bed, I was sick and anxious, my stomach churning all night as a terrible possible future tortured me. I could feel him becoming part of my space, my home, my life.

The next morning, my mother insisted on walking me to school, and I knew it was because she was hoping to see him, and I knew then that I was in real trouble. She was still looking for a replacement for my father and she thought he would do nicely-even though he was so much younger than she was. He had a steady job and he made her laugh. He was her way out of the nine-to-five grind. She didn't have to tell me. I could see it.

'They only dated for a couple of months,' I tell the detectives. 'And then they were in love and he proposed and she was so... happy.' I stop speaking as I think about this. I know now that I was probably the first stepchild he found for himself. I know that he is married to the mother of the young girl who was babysitting the missing child. I know that she is only twelve and I feel a sudden rush of guilt. If I had refused to be silenced all those years ago, maybe I could have saved this child from him. And if that's the case, how many other children were there after me? I was probably the first, and I can imagine him thinking, *My very own young girl, in my very own house. How convenient not to have to leave my chosen victim at school. How wonderful to have her in the house with me.* I don't say this to the detectives, who wait patiently for me to continue speaking as I consider the pretty young girl who was babysitting. I assumed that in this day and age, young girls were fierce and refused to be silenced, but she'd kept his secret, just as we all did. We obviously have a long way to go before women and girls know to always raise their voices.

'After he moved in, he would, he would... all the time. He came into my room at night, into the bathroom when I was in the shower. It was never... it was always just small things. Sometimes I woke up and he was staring down at me and I would see that my top was pushed up, and he would pull it down, almost like a father would, pull it down to make me more comfortable but his hands would brush across my chest. I was never safe, you see,' I tell them. 'There was no safe space for me anywhere, not in school, not at home, not even in my room. Until I started my collections.' Both detectives nod but say nothing. They know what is in my house by now, and a twinge of panic makes me cough. Have the police who have gone through my house disturbed my piles? 'He never left me alone until I started making my piles in my room,' I explain again.

'Yes, we've... Um, can you tell me exactly what you mean by that? What are they for?'

'Piles of ordinary useful things,' I say, eager to explain what keeps me safe now. 'Books and cups and empty glass jars, stones and magazines and cardboard boxes. I piled things up nice and neat, and then...' I start to laugh. I can't help it as I remember the last night he spent in my house, under the same roof as me. I moved a pile of glass jars, stacked in neat rows, higher and higher, right next to my bed, and when he came in, when he tried to get to me, they fell over, clattering and smashing and ringing through the house. The sound of breaking glass brought my mother running to my room, and finally, finally he couldn't deny what he had been doing. He was standing there in his underwear, his face pale in the yellow light that flooded the bedroom when my mother switched it on. He couldn't explain or shift blame or lie.

She didn't even let him speak. She threw him out, tossing his clothes onto the lawn, and then she took me to her bed, where we changed the sheets and she told me she would keep me safe forever. 'Nothing happened,' she kept saying, 'nothing happened,' and I agreed. She was wrong, because so very much had happened, but I agreed so that she would not have to suffer for her choice of man. I agreed and I locked myself out of the world so that I wouldn't have to tell her everything. She would never have to know and we could go on together. I saved my mother but I sacrificed myself and the life I could have had, and she let me. She wasn't perfect, but she loved me, and together we kept the secret from the world and ourselves, even as I collected more and more things to surround myself with and keep me safe and prevent it from ever happening again.

It is too much to explain, so I stop laughing and shake my head. I move from laughter to tears as I think about all the other stepdaughters who were, perhaps, not saved by their mothers.

'All you need to know is that he assaulted me until my mother caught him and that I never really recovered. I couldn't bear to see him hurt another child and that's why I started following him. When I saw what he had done, I was angry at myself for being too late. I knew I needed to expose him to the world, to shout and scream and make people finally, finally listen. I knew that if she went home to him, if Millie was sent home to him, he would hurt her for her whole life. I thought she was his daughter. I didn't realise there was another child. I didn't know that he was hurting another stepchild.'

'Okay, I think that might be enough for now,' says the female detective.

They take me to a cell, where I lie on a bed that smells strange and new and unpleasant, and I pull a blanket around me and try to rest until I can think straight. I can feel some warmth through the small window and I know it will be a beautiful day.

They have not found him, so he is free, free to do this again, and as I close my eyes, I wonder how many other women he has done it to, how many other little girls and women, and how many more he will hurt before they catch him.

SHELBY

EPILOGUE

The spring sunshine bathes the garden in bright yellow light, the blue sky completely cloudless. Shelby looks around at the table covered with food, and the helium-filled balloons in blue and gold bobbing on their strings tied to everything from chairs to table legs to the timber posts on the balcony.

'It looks good, don't you think?' she asks.

'It looks the best,' says Millie. 'And now we're done and we can have a cupcake each.'

Shelby laughs. 'Wait till everyone gets here, Millie!'

'But it's my party,' Millie whines. 'It's my birthday and I'm four.' She holds up four pudgy fingers, making sure that Shelby understands.

'Okay, I tell you what,' says Shelby, crouching down to look at her little sister. 'You can share one cupcake with me, but just one.' They are standing on the stairs of the balcony that comes off the back of the house.

'Yay,' says Millie, and she jumps down the last few stairs to land on the crisp green grass.

'No running,' says Leslie, coming onto the balcony from the

house bearing a tray of fruit cut into shapes. 'I hope they eat this after all the work it took,' she says to Shelby.

'They probably won't,' Shelby replies, 'but we can make smoothies with what's left over in the morning.'

'Good idea,' says Leslie. She walks down the stairs to place the tray on the table, and then she stands and watches as Millie looks at the plate of cupcakes, making sure to choose the best one, explaining to Leslie that she and Shelby are going to share one. Leslie takes the cupcake off the plate and hands it to her. 'No running,' she says again, as Millie darts back up the stairs to Shelby. The cupcake is delicious, and Shelby laughs at the blue icing that coats her sister's lips.

Summer is just around the corner, and she and Millie are excited for the school holidays and the beach house their father has rented for a whole month. 'Right on the beach, just us and the sand and nothing else,' he told them.

'And no work,' Leslie said.

'And no work,' he agreed.

Leslie said she could bring a friend, but Shelby doesn't want to be with anyone except her family. She is not talking to Kiera, and she hopes that the rumours that Kiera is going to a different high school next year are true. She doesn't want to speak to her ever again. She plans to be more careful about choosing friends in the future.

Shelby will only be spending three weeks at the house, because she has agreed to one week with her mother, who is serving her sentence in the community. She has to do hours and hours at the local community centre and she is not allowed to leave the state for two years. She has to check in with the police as well, something that Shelby knows she hates. But she knew. She knew and she did nothing as Leslie and her father grew frantic and Shelby felt sick with guilt. She did nothing as people searched the park and the neighbourhood and more and more police got involved. She did nothing except protect Trevor and herself.

After Trevor had picked up Millie and run from the house, he called his wife and she told him to leave the little girl in the park, told him to just dump her and leave. The idea was that he would find her and be hailed a hero. But Ruth stepped in and prevented that plan from going ahead.

Ruth is an unusual woman, nervous and unsure, but Shelby feels a connection with her, because Ruth really understands what it's like to have been touched in a way that felt wrong and yet to have to question yourself for the way you are feeling. She and Ruth have talked a little and she hopes they will be able to speak more. Shelby likes her psychologist, but only Ruth completely gets it.

Too many people know what happened to Shelby but don't understand it. It's made school awkward and she has a lot of angry moments, especially at her mother. She can't get over the lies and the deception. She refused to speak to Bianca for nearly two months. But one night she was sitting next to Leslie in her bed and Leslie said, 'You never want to regret a decision like this. See her, let her explain or apologise, let her speak. And then you can decide. I can't forgive her, but she's not my mother, and I know that she will never forgive herself. She was... I don't know how to explain it, but I do know that men like Trevor can convince even the strongest person to believe them. He was very good at explaining away what he did, at blaming other people and shifting the focus away from himself. She was kind of lost, your mother, lost and sad because she was so in love with him, and she did something terrible and crazy. But I also know from what she said in court that she is filled with regret. So maybe give her a chance to explain and then make a decision on whether or not you want to see her.'

Shelby had agreed and had started seeing her mother. But something is missing. Something will always be missing. She can never trust her again. But she has her father, and she has Leslie and Millie. She has a family and that's the best she can hope for. She will spend time with her mother, but Bianca will never really mother her again. That's okay, though, because she has a stepmother, and those four letters at the beginning of the word don't make her less to Shelby, not at all.

Last week she had been in the middle of a fight with Leslie over not handing in a project, and she had gotten so angry she had shouted, 'Stop telling me what to do, you're not my—'

'Don't you dare,' Leslie had yelled back. 'I *am* your mother... I am your mother, Shelby. You have two mothers. Two.' And that had made Shelby cry, because she felt it was true, it really was. Leslie helped her finish the project after that, and the artwork was so good, she got an A.

'Look, look,' shouts Millie now, distracting Shelby from thoughts of anything else, 'the bouncy castle is going up!'

Shelby lifts her little sister up and together they watch as the pink princess castle takes shape.

'Up it goes,' says Shelby, as Millie winds her arms around her neck. 'Up it goes.'

LESLIE

When people start arriving, Leslie gives up telling Millie not to run. She is too excited as she shows her friends the craft table and the face painting station, where a lovely young woman with tumbling blonde curls sits ready to do whatever design a child requests. Millie has a blue and gold butterfly covering her whole face and she keeps running back to the face painter to ask for another look in the hand mirror, making sure her butterfly is still in place.

Millie is supposed to be calm and quiet and sedate, according to her doctors, but there is no way Leslie can tell her four-year-old child to stop doing things that feel good. Looking at her, it's impossible to tell that she was unconscious for three days after an operation to stop the bleeding on her brain, that they had no idea who she would be when she woke up or what she would be capable of; that they had no idea if she would wake up at all.

Her hair is short but styled to cover the patch where the doctors had to shave it to get to the bleed. Leslie pastes a smile on her face for the partygoers and shudders at the thought of her child on an operating table. 'I'll fly in the best surgeon in the world. We'll get the best care. I don't care what it costs,' Randall had told her, desperate to somehow control an uncontrollable situation. But she knew that the care they were getting for their daughter was the best they could get. She knew that there was nothing more they could do.

Leslie stayed with her child. She only left the hospital once a day, to go home and shower and change her clothes, leaving Randall with his daughter. Even as she slept, she was alert to any changes in Millie's breathing, any noises in the room. She had grown used to feeling as though she was forever moving underwater, her brain struggling to catch up with what was going on. Randall kept trying to feed her, to bring her things to tempt her to eat, but food was a struggle as she watched her daughter being kept alive with tubes. Food was a struggle for her and for Shelby, who was, Leslie had been able to see, weighed down by her guilt and dealing with her mother's betrayal.

'I worry for her,' Leslie told Randall one night, as they sat by Millie's bedside and the clock moved towards midnight.

'She'll wake up, Les, she will,' he said, repeating the same thing he had been saying since their daughter's operation.

'Not Millie. I mean... Millie, well, it's more than worry. I worry for Shelby. She's carrying too much for a twelve-year-old. We need to get her some help.'

Randall had agreed and Leslie thinks the young woman Shelby agreed to speak to has helped. She hopes that she continues helping.

And then, at last, Millie opened her eyes, a day, a moment that will never leave Leslie. In her mind it will always hold the same space as the memory of Millie's birth, a time when everything suddenly changed.

It was a Thursday afternoon, the wind howling outside the window of the warm hospital room, and Shelby was sitting next to Millie's bed, reading to her from *Matilda* by Roald Dahl.

Shelby's voice went up and down as she voiced the different characters, as though she were in front of a whole audience of children instead of just one silent child. Leslie was dozing in her chair, listening to the story and the soft beeps from the machine monitoring Millie's heart.

'And that's the end of Chapter Ten,' said Shelby, and she put down the book and took a sip from her water bottle.

'I'm also thirsty,' came a little voice, and Leslie opened her eyes and leapt out of her chair all at the same time. 'Millie,' she said, standing over her daughter, stroking her hair. 'Millie, Millie, Millie,' she repeated, while Shelby ran for the door.

'Please come,' Shelby called to a passing nurse, her voice filled with panicked excitement. 'She's awake, my sister is awake.'

The nurse had darted into the room and over to the bed, her hands on Millie's head and arms and then her wrist. 'Just a moment,' she said gently, and Leslie had stepped back, felt Shelby next to her and hugged her tightly while the doctor was called and he examined Millie.

'Can you tell me how many fingers I'm holding up?' he asked, holding up two fingers.

Millie looked confused for a moment and Leslie felt her heart drop, but then her little girl smiled. 'Two,' she said, 'and Shelby told me two plus two is four. I'm going to be four on my next birthday and Mummy says I can have a jumping castle.'

The doctor laughed and Leslie said, 'You can have whatever you want, Millie Molly, whatever you want.'

She had called Randall, crying so hard he had assumed the worst, until Shelby took the phone and explained and Leslie heard her husband's hoarse shouts of joy fill the room.

And now they are here, and Millie, sensing that she will be denied nothing, has asked for a party filled with everything. Leslie watches her showing a friend the different kinds of glitter they have. It will appear everywhere for weeks, she knows, but she doesn't care. Nothing matters but that her daughter is safe and well and happy. As she looks over at Shelby, who is sternly supervising the craft table, she whispers, 'Nothing matters except that both my daughters are safe.'

'Oh Les,' says Randall softly, coming up behind her. 'You're just... you're the best human being I know.' He puts his arms around her waist. 'Aren't we the lucky ones?' he says.

'Yes,' agrees Leslie, 'we really are.'

She is working on forgiveness at the moment, on forgiving Bianca for what she did, but she's not getting very far. In court, she had seen a human being diminished. Bianca had lost weight and her lovely blonde hair was greasy and thin.

'I loved him,' was all she could say, and 'I'm so sorry, so sorry.' Randall had watched his ex-wife, his arms crossed and his jaw set.

They have both been profoundly shocked by what happened. Bianca never knew what Trevor was doing to Shelby, and in her more gracious moments, Leslie tries to believe that she would have left him if she had known. Life and love are complicated, and sometimes a mother has to wonder if she should save her child or herself. It would never be a dilemma for Leslie, but maybe things were too hard for Bianca, maybe that skewed everything. She still can't forgive her, and she doesn't feel she should have to.

She cannot think about Trevor. He is still out there, still free, and sometimes she will be in a shopping centre and catch a glimpse of a man with curly blonde hair and a build like his, and her heart will hammer in her chest. If Millie is with her, she will clutch her tightly, too tightly for her daughter, who will complain, 'Let go, Mum.' The police are still looking for him, and Constable Dickerson has assured her that they will not give up on finding him and bringing him to justice.

Leslie is struggling to let go even a little, struggling to trust that her daughter will be safe at home without her, struggling to trust anyone with her, but she's trying. Last week Shelby babysat for a couple of hours on Saturday night. She texted Leslie every twenty minutes, updating her, until finally Leslie told her to relax. Shelby is struggling to trust herself, which is somehow worse.

They will both get there, she's sure of it, because she and Randall really want to move on and they want to help Shelby too. She wants this family to be a unit: them against the world.

On days like today, it is impossible to believe that Millie nearly died. Nearly, nearly…

'Come and jump, Mum, come and jump in the castle with me and Shelby,' shouts Millie, grabbing her hand. And Leslie laughs and follows her daughters into the castle that reaches to the sky, where children are giggling.

Nearly, nearly… but here she is. Leslie holds hands with her daughters and together they bounce in the castle, their bodies flying through the air as they nearly, nearly touch the sky.

RUTH

I have been sitting in my car for twenty minutes now, watching the children and the parents arrive, each child clutching a brightly wrapped present for Millie. I want to get out of the car so desperately, but fear is keeping me stuck here.

'We would love it if you could come,' Leslie had said on the phone when she called to invite me. People can be surprising creatures. I assumed that Leslie and her family would never want to see me again. I was dumbfounded when Randall hired a lawyer, a tall woman with her hair in a bun and a beautifully tailored suit, to represent me.

'You thought you were saving her from Trevor,' Randall said when I asked why he'd done it. 'And you've had your struggles... You weren't trying to hurt her.'

'She could have died,' I told him. By then I had apologised so many times, written Leslie and Shelby and Randall emails and sent text messages. I didn't know what else to do. But this family, this wonderful family, have forgiven me.

I received a suspended sentence for interfering with a police investigation and withholding evidence. The kidnap charge was dropped quickly and my history, my sad little history, which has kept me imprisoned in my house surrounded by my neat piles, was taken into account. The shame of hearing what he had done to me, what I had allowed my life to become because of him, forced me to hang my head as the lawyer spoke to the judge. I couldn't look at people as decisions about my life were made. I was once again powerless and a child, but at the same time there was a flutter of relief inside me. I was not hiding any more.

I am required to see a psychologist once a week, and while I never imagined that talking about what happened would help, it does seem to. I don't have to keep the secret any more. Instead, I tell Jenny everything, everything, and it is the telling that has helped.

Last week I cleared out the living room in my house. It was hard. I felt exposed and raw and as though I couldn't breathe, but I gave Jenny a call and she talked to me until I felt calmer, safer. I have also begun looking for a job, preferably one that involves an office or a safe space. But I'm looking.

I go to the coffee shop where I first saw him every day. I need to check that he is not there, that he has not returned to terrorise me again. I know he won't. He has run far from here, just like he did after my mother caught him, and then again after he was caught by someone at the last school he taught at. But still, I go to check.

The owner of the coffee shop, a man named Lance, recognises me now and calls out, 'Hello, Ruth, the usual?' as I walk in. He's given me a lift home a few times when the spring rain has been persistent. He drives a silly sports car, an incongruous purple Porsche, and the first time he gave me a lift, I had to hold my breath because the mess on the floor, the collections of wrappers and old drink bottles, made me feel edgy and unsafe. When he offered a lift again, I wanted to say no thank you, but I saw how much he wanted to help me get home in the storm.

The car was neat and shiny inside then. 'I know you don't like mess,' he told me. 'I could see it.'

'I don't mind if it's neatly stacked... anything, just as long as it's neat,' I explained.

'All right then,' he said.

Yesterday he asked me to try a new cake he was thinking of adding to the menu, and we sat and chatted for a bit. He's single, divorced with no children, but he has two dogs. He's asked me to come and meet them, and I think I will, I really think I will.

The street is quiet now, all the children having arrived, but I can hear shrieks of laughter from the garden at the back of the house.

You can do this, Ruth, I tell myself. And before I can think about it anymore, I open the door and walk towards the house, clutching the present I bought for Millie. It's a nail polish set. When she was in my house, lying on the bed in my old room, I sometimes went in to hold her little hand, stroke her soft skin and run my fingertips over her smooth blue nails with the gold stripe. I hope she likes her present.

The front door is standing open, and I follow the noise to the back of the house.

I see Shelby first, her blonde hair tied up, a dab of glitter on her cheek and a drink in her hand. 'Ruth,' she shouts, 'come over here, come and help with the crafts.'

I place the present on the table filled with gifts as Leslie waves at me from behind the food table and Randall calls, 'Hey, hi,' from near the jumping castle.

You can do this, Ruth, I remind myself as I go and take my place at the craft table next to Millie, who beams her beautiful smile at me.

You can do this.

TREVOR

The small coffee shop sits on the edge of the tiny coastal town. There are only five tables inside, but outside in the sunshine, the pavement is filled with people enjoying the heat.

Inside, a woman and her daughter are sharing a piece of caramel cheesecake.

'That guy has been looking at you, Mum,' says the girl.

Her mother flushes slightly. 'I'm sure he's not.' She glances at the man her daughter is talking about and sees that he is indeed looking over at her. He smiles and she smiles back, admiring his broad shoulders and blonde hair. He's nice-looking, with blue eyes.

'It's been ages since the divorce, Mum, and I'm thirteen now. You really should start dating again.'

'Oh, I don't know,' says her mother, her hand reaching up to push her hair back behind her ears.

The man starts to stand up, maintaining eye contact.

'He's coming over here, he's coming over here,' whispers the girl, excitement in her voice.

As he steps towards their table, two policewomen enter the coffee shop. They walk towards the man, though he is concentrating on the mother and the girl so he doesn't see them. He doesn't notice the policewomen until one of them puts a hand on his shoulder. 'Trevor Richards?' she says.

The man turns, panic in his eyes. 'I'm not...' he says.

'Tony Richardson,' says the other constable, and the man turns scarlet to the tips of his ears. 'We are placing you under arrest on the charge of sexual assault of a minor, kidnapping and grievous bodily harm.'

The mother stands up.

'I haven't finished my cake,' says the daughter, fascinated by what she's watching.

'We'll take it to go,' says the mother firmly, and she leads her daughter out of the coffee shop and into the sunshine for a walk on the beach.

'Weird,' says the daughter after a few minutes. 'Imagine if you'd started dating him or something.'

'Yes,' says the mother, 'imagine.'

A LETTER FROM NICOLE

Dear Reader,

I would like to thank you so much for taking the time to read *The Stepchild*. If you enjoyed it, and want to keep up to date with all my latest releases, just sign up at the following link. Your email address will never be shared and you can unsubscribe at any time.

www.bookouture.com/nicole-trope

Ruth has been added to my list of favourite characters I've written. She is a woman who, as a child, was damaged and hurt by all the adults in her life. And yet she is still trying to find a way to be in the world. Her character simply appeared one day – as did her need for collecting ordinary useful things. Her piles of stuff protected her from everything, and now that she feels safer, I hope that she manages to find a way forward and maybe even find love.

When writing about sexual assault, it is shocking to think that there are few women on the planet who have not been subjected to some form of it. The small touches, dirty jokes, hands that wander just a little may not seem like a big deal, but we are all scarred by remaining silent, by believing we should remain silent.

The #MeToo movement has shone a very bright light on

things that many women felt they simply had to accept, and still do. We have a long way to go.

It is also always important to remember that good men are everywhere, that our fathers, brothers, husbands and sons are good men capable of changing the way things have been done for generations.

I'm so happy that Randall and Leslie have managed to make Shelby feel safe again, and that she has a loving family to support her. I think Shelby and Millie will be close forever, supporting each other as they grow up.

It's sad that Shelby will not be able to really forgive her mother, but at least she is allowing contact. Bianca was a lonely, sad, angry woman and she is trying to make amends for her terrible mistakes.

If you have enjoyed this novel, it would be so appreciated if you could take the time to leave a review. I read them all and find it wonderful when readers relate to the characters I write about.

I would also love to hear from you. You can find me on Facebook and Twitter and I'm always happy to connect with readers.

Thanks again for reading

Nicole x

facebook.com/NicoleTrope

twitter.com/nicoletrope

instagram.com/nicoletropeauthor

ACKNOWLEDGEMENTS

I would like to thank Christina Demosthenous for her encouraging, lovely support and her unwavering belief in my abilities. However difficult things got in the last two crazy years, I was always assured of her focus and attention. I never question whether she wants the best for my work and for me – I absolutely trust she does.

Thank you to Victoria Blunden for her insightful first edit.

I would also like to thank Sarah Hardy for all her hard work in spreading the word about this novel. Thanks to the whole team at Bookouture, including Alexandra Holmes and Lizzie Brien.

Thanks to Jane Selley for the copyedit and Liz Hatherell for the proofread.

Thanks to my mother, Hilary, for reading every time and on time.

Thanks also to David, Mikhayla, Isabella and Jacob – just for being there.

And once again thank you to those who read, review, blog about my work and contact me on Facebook or Twitter to let me know you loved a novel. Every message means more than you can know.

Made in United States
Troutdale, OR
04/10/2025

30492373R00148